MW00782004

THE NIGHTMARE KING

FALL ASLEEP AND WAIT FOR ME

KAT BLACKTHORNE

DARK HEARTS PRESS

Cover by Occult Goddess

Edits by Krys

Proofreading by Cassidy Hudspeth

Formatting by Kat Blackthorne

For the ones so haunted they only find peace in sleep. May your nightmare find you. May you always awaken to days brighter than your darkest nights.

PREFACE

This is not a romance.
What you are about to read is a nightmare...
most love stories are.

Content warnings include:

  Death

  Trauma

  Mental health

  Horror

  Knives

  Knife play

  Axes

  Zombies

  Violence

  Pain

  Broken glass/wood

Blood

Blood play

Sexual content

Sexual use of medical equipment

Masks

Drowning

Heights

Therapy

Medication

Depression

Attempted SA

Body gore

Body horror

Car accident

Witchcraft

Graphic nightmares

Please read with caution to protect your mental health.
Please visit https://988lifeline.org/ for crisis resources.

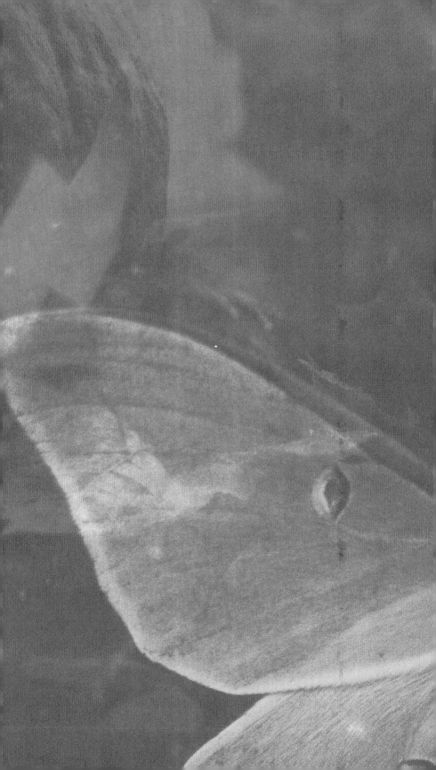

PROLOGUE

SOMETHING WICKED

Halloween was the one time of year when everyone looked as crazed and weird on the outside as I felt on the inside year-round. That's why it was my favorite holiday and why I stumbled through an overcast maze of pumpkins. My friends had long abandoned me, and the autumn chill froze through my flannel as I wove through the stacks of orange gourds. How they were all balanced so perfectly and kept growing larger and larger, I didn't stop to question.

Thunder clapped in the distance, though no raindrops fell. Dread crept into my psyche as I rubbed my arms for warmth. Suddenly, I felt truly and disturbingly alone. Hoping I was going the right way, I turned a corner, pushing past the corn stalks interspersed within the maze, and reached a clearing— the center of the maze.

A long figure stood abnormally tall and looming as the

sky grew dark behind him. Black against orange, the perfect and most terrifying Halloween scene.

He stood on a thick, skeletal body, haphazardly draped in torn fabric, and cocked his pumpkin head. "Well, look at that. I found you."

I swallowed my scream and turned to run, but the path behind me had closed.

Shutting my eyes as tightly as I could, I hoped and prayed the darkness would offer some sort of escape. To my horror, I felt his warm breath on the back of my ear and smelt cinnamon and pumpkin spice as he whispered. "Time to wake up. Time to let go."

That sequence would repeat itself for weeks before I even became aware that it was a dream. Once I finally caught on, the fear never left but I began to talk to the pumpkin man... and he talked back.

It was the beginning and the end of everything.

Another night just like the others. The crow cawed. Thunder clapped. I reached the end of the maze, and he pulled me into his embrace. Only now, through the fear there was a strange comfort. I recognized his violet gaze when he stroked a bone finger over my cheek. There was this form, and there was the man form. I liked them both. I liked any nightmare where he found me.

That's the thing about becoming aware of your dreams as you're inside them, though, you become startlingly aware that they'll end at any moment.

This is the tragic beginning of my end.

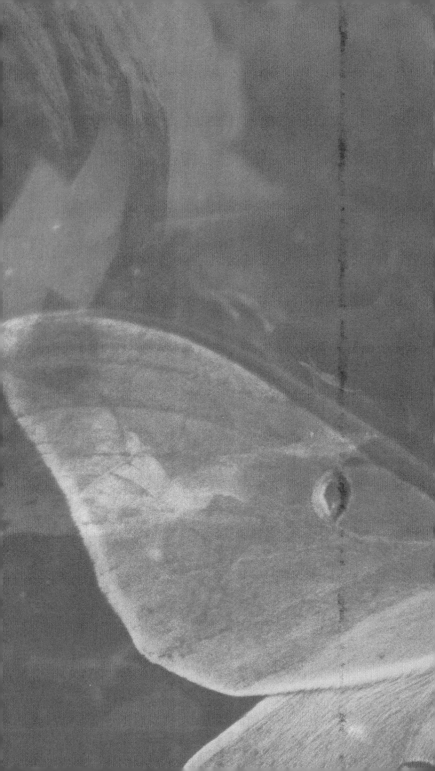

O sleep, O gentle sleep, Nature's soft nurse, how have I frightened thee, that thou no more will weigh my eyelids down, and steep my senses in forgetfulness?

William Shakespeare

Halloween was the one time of year when everyone looked as crazed and weird on the outside as I felt on the inside year-round. That's why it was my favorite holiday and why I stumbled through an overcast maze of pumpkins. My friends had long abandoned me, and the autumn chill froze through my flannel as I wove through the stacks of orange gourds. How they were all balanced so perfectly and kept growing larger and larger, I didn't stop to question.

Thunder clapped in the distance, though no raindrops fell.

Oh, here we go again.

Trepidation crept into my being as I rubbed my arms for warmth. Suddenly knew I wasn't alone. I knew I was going the right way, I turned a corner, pushing past the corn stalks interspersed within the maze, and reached a clearing— the center of the maze where I knew I'd find him.

A long figure stood abnormally tall and looming as the sky grew dark behind him. Black against orange, the perfect and most terrifying Halloween scene.

He stood on a thick, skeletal body, haphazardly draped in torn fabric, and cocked his pumpkin head. "Well, I found you again."

I swallowed my scream and turned to run, but the path behind me had closed.

Shutting my eyes as tightly as I could, I hoped and prayed the darkness would offer some sort of escape. To my horror, I felt his warm breath on the back of my ear and smelt cinnamon and pumpkin spice as he whispered. "Time to wake up. Time to let go."

The crow cawed. Thunder clapped. I reached the end of the maze, and he pulled me into his embrace. Only now, through the fear there was a strange comfort. I recognized his violet gaze when he stroked a bone finger over my cheek. There was this form, and there was the man form. I liked them both. I liked any nightmare where he found me. That's the thing about becoming aware of your dreams as you're inside them, though. You become startlingly aware that they'll end at any moment.

"You aren't real!" I bellowed into the fog of the maze.

In a flash of dark shadow, the back of his palm smacked my cheek. My teeth chattered, and my skin burned from the contact. Shock and horror bolted through me. His gaze was a hateful mix of passion and anger as something in his jaw ticked.

Pain was a new addition to the same nightmare.

"Did that feel *unreal*, Lilac?"

My lower lip quivered as the overwhelming urge to cry washed over me. Not because he'd hit me, but because he wasn't real, couldn't be real, and I'd wake up at any moment just like I always did.

He stepped forward as if striding out of his pumpkin head and skeleton costume. The air around us swirled with purple and black smoke. The pumpkin man was terrifying... this man was, too, only this form was devastatingly hand-some. A dark knight that could only be conjured in a dream. Taking my chin between his fingers he tilted my head up. "Kiss me and let me show you what else *real* feels like, oh, sleeper."

I nodded, feeling warm tears stain the burning cheek in the wake of his palm. I felt it. I felt this, somehow, even though I knew I was asleep.

Groaning into his strong, firm body, his lips brushed my own, parting my mouth and flicking his tongue against mine. This phantom of my dreams tasted like maple and salt and sex.

We'd fallen into this same dance over and over again. Sometimes, small details would change, but one thing remained: each time, I'd wake in sorrow that he wasn't real and worry that I'd never see him again. That this figment of my imagination would disappear like water through my fingers. Because we can't conjure our own dreams, as hard as I'd tried on the nights he didn't visit me, I couldn't make him appear. Which made this lucid nightmare all the more addictive.

The phantom's palm pressed against my lower belly, sinking between my thighs. My core burned with want as I came apart with only one quick and firm touch. Forgetting for a moment who I was in real life, letting go of my true reality and breathing into blissful oblivion.

In sleep, I could die.

Sleep was death without the mess, the guilt, the commitment. If I slept the day away the day didn't exist, I missed nothing, I felt nothing.

When I was awake, I longed for sleep while simultaneously hating everything—I felt everything.

Staring at the outdated ceiling fan, I steadied my breathing. My inner thighs slick with my desire and release, my core still pulsing from the dream, the nightmare—him. My right cheek was still warm, and I rubbed it softly if only to touch an imaginary piece of him left behind. I could try to go back to sleep, and I would have if my stomach weren't tight with hunger.

My therapist's chant echoed through my mind.

Just focus on the next thing.
Every step forward is a win.
Do small things to take care of yourself.
Assess whether this is a low, medium, or high day.

Morning checklist for a medium day:
Sit up.
Take my medicine.
Use the bathroom.
Wash my face.
Brush my teeth.
Eat breakfast.

MY HAND only slightly trembled as I unscrewed the prescription lid. The morning checklist was only slightly overwhelming. The urge to pull my blanket over my head and go back to sleep slowly slipped away, sliding down my throat with my little pink pill.

If I completed my checklists, I'd be extra tired. I could go to bed early, and maybe I'd see him again. That thought, that hope, would propel me toward another repetitive day in the waking world.

Sugar cereal, caffeinated coffee, (which my psychologist told me not to have but I did anyway), pepped me up enough to clock in only five minutes late at work. My apron wasn't too heavy or tight, and the organic grocery store was slow.

Bananas were code 4011 and then weighed. Unless they were organic, those were 94011. But sometimes, if a customer was really nice, I'd weigh them as standard because that was cheaper.

"Hey, Lucy. Watch party for The Walking Dead at my place tonight. You coming?" Brandon abandoned his register and took post at my bagging station. A nice gesture, but I didn't really mind bagging the groceries, it was the talking to the people I didn't like.

I adjusted my name tag. "Zombies aren't really my thing. Plus, hasn't that series been off the air for years now? I think I know how it ends already."

"Don't be such a Debbie-downer. We're starting from episode one and watching one a week. I know I'd love to see you."

Brandon wasn't terrible to look at. Tall and stout with sandy blond hair. If I were normal, maybe I would be attracted to him. Maybe if my dopamine weren't broken, him asking me out would have given me butterflies. If my serotonin wasn't store-bought, I bet him brushing my hand as he reached to refill my receipt paper would have made me giddy. But it did none of those things. Instead, my thoughts wandered to the nightmare man, and I calculated the hours until I could go back to sleep.

"You got somewhere to be?" Brandon pressed. "I noticed

you're checking the clock. Or maybe you just want me to go away..."

"No," I answered. "I mean, yes, I have to be home early tonight for my other job. Sorry."

His brow furrowed in either hurt or confusion. I rubbed the back of my neck, feeling a pang of guilt. My therapist would praise me if I went out with people my age, and praise from my therapist would feel nice. "Next week?" I asked. "Raincheck?"

Brandon flashed an accomplished smile as he ripped open a new container of paper bags and stocked my station. "It's a date."

No, the only date I had was with my mattress and stuffed animals. The only wishing I did was to see him again. Would I remember to ask him questions this time? Would he even answer if I did? Dream world wasn't like real life. Everything was hazier, my mind was fuzzy, and some-times I remembered who I was and that I was dreaming. Sometimes I didn't.

I think the nightmare man liked it better when I didn't.

My name was Lucy, but he called me Lilac. I liked Lilac better.

Therapy was normal. Dr. Truman checked my lists and walked me through a meditative breathing exercise that I actually hated but pretended to love because it meant we didn't have to talk. And the clock ticked down, down... it was almost dark by the time I got home. A full day out, *not* in bed, *not* in the apartment. The accomplishment swelled in my chest. For a medium day, I did pretty freaking good.

A full water bottle with ice and a plate of rice, chicken, and vegetables awaited me in front of my open laptop in the living room. "Half of an unsold cake in the fridge for you, too. But eat the zucchini, Lucy, don't just push it around your plate." My sister bit into an apple and pinched the blinds. "This apartment complex is well-lit at night, at least. Not like you're going anywhere, but still."

My throat warmed in irritation. "I actually have a party to go to next week, and it's at night, so, maybe you don't know everything about me, Sam."

It was rude, I was rude, especially as I bit into the first hot meal I'd had in days. She knew that if she didn't cook for me that I wouldn't bother to eat more than a bag of chips. This was her thing, I guessed. Sam rolled her eyes. "I'll believe it when I see it. Your location on your phone is turned on, right?"

"Don't you have a six-year-old's birthday cake to bake or something? My show is almost on."

She checked the time before shutting my blinds for me and placing a hand on her hip in expectation.

I sighed. "Thank you for, you know, whatever. But I could cook for myself if I had... supplies."

"No way, take that up with Doctor Truman. No sharps." Her expression softened as I avoided her pitying gaze, clicking play on my laptop. "Here for you, kid, whether you like it or not." She kissed the top of my head, and I swatted her away. "My ringer is on. Text if you need me."

"I *don't* need you," I scoffed as she closed the door, using her key to lock it behind her. The key she had made and I never actually gave her. God, my sister was annoying. And ever since what happened— she'd been like this. An over-protective pest.

I *didn't* need her. She wanted me to need her, but I didn't. I'd been living on my own for months and doing just fine. There was one blurry, singular incident of sorts that no one would talk to me about, and wham-bam-Sam took it upon herself to mother-smother me multiple times a week. I felt like a hamster in a cage. Her pet bunny. Sam stopped by to refill my water bottle and leave carrots. It was patronizing and stupid, and I wanted to tell her to get a life of her own and stop meddling in mine.

My life was fine. I had my systems in place, my head-phones blaring loud music and books, the televison on all night, the stereo in my car, my shows queued up and ready to watch, work with its constant stream of scanning beeps and bagging and cart retrieving.

I had my checklists.

Do my checklists.

Go to work.

Watch TV.

But then my favorite part of the day was after that. My reward. This was a science now. I knew what to do. I knew I needed to be the perfect amount of tired for him to find me.

Not over tired, not hyped-up awake. Moderately sleepy stacked the odds in my favor. As I watched my shows, I found my box of supplies under the sofa and tinkered with my jewelry. My second job, what I wished was my main job. Maybe someday I'd complete a collection and get the balls to approach shops to display my works.

My fingers ached after over an hour of toying with loop rings and connecting charms to necklace chains. I liked silver lately, and lots of mismatched dangling charms. Maybe I would keep it for myself, though, I never wore my own creations anymore.

The time on my laptop blinked ten at night and my heart fluttered as I blew through my evening checklist.

Medium Evening Checklist
Lock doors
Turn off lights
Brush Teeth
Lay out the next day's clothes

Those basic activities didn't feel so difficult that evening, though fatigue pulled at my eyelids as I haphazardly tossed jeans and a t-shirt onto the stool at the foot of my bed. Checklist done, I'd made it through another ordinary, boring, stupid day. Now my escape, now my reward. Everything in my life was carefully charted, planned out, and monitored. There were no surprises, nothing out of the mundane ever happened. I did the same thing every day, spoke to the same people, and went about the same routine. Except when I went to bed... moths erupted in my stomach at the fantasies of past dreams as they flitted through my mind. The tantalizing excitement of having something to wonder about, not knowing, the hope of seeing him again... the feeling was unmatched by anything the real world could offer me.

Not everyone had a phantom in their dreams.

I was special.

I hoped he would come as drowsiness pulled me into its grip.

Thank the stars, thank the heavens and hells... sleep wasn't the only thing that found me that night.

CHAPTER
TWO
HELLO, NIGHTMARE

How blessed are some people, whose lives have no fears,
no dreads, to whom sleep is a blessing that comes
nightly, and brings nothing but sweet dreams.

Bram Stoker

A cobblestone walkway was cold and rough under my bare feet as a sea breeze tangled through my hair. I swallowed and felt something tight around my ribs. A corset perched above a billowing skirt. I was on some sort of boat dock. I startled when gulls squawked overhead. This was a nice break from the pumpkin maze. I did love being by the water, if only in a dream. I could feel the muggy salt breeze on my skin. Were everyone's dreams this real?

Or maybe...

I wandered down the path, wondering why he never

gave me shoes—wondering how it was possible that I stepped on a pebble and it pricked my heel. This town was quaint and smelled like ocean brine. Two men stumbled out of a pub, tipping their hats at me as I went inside the bustling establishment. My feet stuck to the floor, feeling the spilled beer and cigar ash between my toes as I shimmied onto a barstool, already annoyed at the surplus of fabric strapped against my body. This was different, he'd never brought me here before. Or maybe I'd gotten lost, what if he didn't come? My heart sank.

"Water for the lady?" a bartender asked, drying a pint glass. "I'm George, by the way."

"Sure—"

"I don't want no trouble!"

I startled as he shouted, looking over my shoulder. "We're the only place on the eastern seaboard that even still serves your kind—don't blow it, *pirate*."

The aroma of moss and rum enveloped me as he took his seat next to me, tipping his black pirate's hat. "Evening, Lilac."

My palms were slick against the countertop, and I dried them on my skirt, trying to compose my thoughts, to ease the flutter of emotions that bubbled in my chest. "Hello, *Nightmare*."

The bartender glared before sliding me a cup of water and busying himself pouring my companion a beer. Then it felt like a dream, as I looked at him, I knew it was impossible anyone in real life could be as stunning as he was. With jet black, slicked back hair, sharp jawline, and piercing violet stare—he didn't exist—couldn't truly exist. My throat tightened.

"None of that," he admonished. "And no *dates* with shop clerks either."

I narrowed my gaze. "How did you know about that?"

He ran a lazy finger over the lid of his glass. "You're all he thinks about. He imagines you in your ripped jeans and that pink top. Cliché, if you ask me, I much prefer this darling little number."

"This corset hurts," I answered, hiding my grin.

"Good."

My cheeks flushed, and my eyes dropped to his full lips. "You look nice as a pirate," I whispered.

"I do, don't I? Thought the leather vest was quite dashing, myself." He downed his beer with a few chugs before grabbing my barstool and pulling it closer. I gasped, feeling my body press to his. My mind worried about the bartender, who watched on with judgment.

"Tell me what troubles you, oh, sleeper." His lips lightly grazed mine, stealing my breath, sending jolts of passion through my body, crashing into my core like waves on the nearby beach.

My words caught in my throat. "You—you know what."

He growled against my neck, giving it a bite that stung and nearly broke the skin. "Not this *you aren't real* nonsense again."

"None of this... it's all too good. I know I'll wake up—"

Swirls of violet, mirroring the shade of his deep stare swirled around us as he picked me up and put me on the bar counter. He separated my legs with his wide body and grabbed my chin. "Stop worrying, Lilac. Feel me, enjoy me."

He pulled up my skirt before placing his pirate hat on my head and disappearing under my dress. I moaned at the feel of his mouth on my center, looking around the bar, but we were shrouded in smoke, and no one paid us any mind. "Such anxiety plagues you, oh, sleeper. Can't you not even be free in your dreams?"

His tongue swept against my clit, making me groan at the wet feel of him. "God, you feel so real."

"And you taste like the finest of wines," he murmured against my center. "Perhaps the seaside vexes you," he mused, pushing me to the top of my release. "Tomorrow, I shall find us a better spot."

My moan was silenced by screams, as shots rang out. My body tightened and fluttered against the aftershocks of my orgasm as my lover stood, planting a slick kiss on my lips. The bartender pulled out a shotgun, firing at the doorway as patrons screamed. My nightmare's violet eyes lingered for a moment on mine, as if he wanted to say something, but stopped himself. "I must go."

Chairs clattered to the ground as the shrieking persisted. The nightmare portion of the dream was here, the scary parts, the frightening end.

He made to pull back, but I grabbed onto his vest, and he

stopped, just as I felt myself slipping away. "Let me stay with you?"

I'd never asked that before.

Something flashed across his stare, and his jaw hardened. With a sigh, he planted a small kiss on my cheek and whispered. "Away with you."

THREE

AWAKE

I believe in everything until it's disproved. So I believe in fairies, the myths, dragons. It all exists, even if it's in your mind. Who's to say that dreams and nightmares aren't as real as the here and now?

John Lennon

I forced my eyes closed, refusing to open them, and coercing myself back into a slumber of nothingness. Rest, biological, mundane. It was too short, too quick. I could still feel the pricking of the corset against my waist, the sticky floor on my feet. The feeling of his violet eyes roaming my body and his tongue swiping against my bare skin. How I wished to roll over and see him in bed beside me.

He'd never been a pirate before, though, it suited him.

He was always dramatically vague, swashbuckling his way through my pleasure and pain.

My therapist should know about him, about this. I'd googled it, already, and read all about delusions. If Sam knew, she would wrinkle her forehead to fight the tears, fumbling through the realization that her baby sister was losing her mind—truly—losing grip on reality. While my therapist and doctors would... I don't know what they'd do. No, I couldn't tell them. And what harm was this odd fantasy adventure? So maybe I was dreaming, but it gave me a reason to get through the day if only a longing for the night. For a chance to see him again. A pirate, a pumpkin phantom, a regular guy—whatever adornments, whatever setting shift, it was always him and me.

My fixation, my mirage, my dark shadow man.

* * *

Doctor Truman yawned and scratched his grey beard. "I apologize, I didn't rest well last night. Speaking of—how is your sleep, Lucy?"

The question was cold water splashed on my face and I fumbled over my words, watching the clock as I did. "Normal, totally fine and normal. Why?"

"Your medications can interfere with sleep. Lack of rest can make your symptoms worse. You said you're having more average days lately, that makes me hopeful we're on the right path with your prescriptions and the EMDR."

I fidgeted with the corner of a pillow on the therapy couch. "Could the medicine be making... dreams more vivid?"

The doctor paused the tapping of his pen. "It could. Why? Are you experiencing vivid dreams?"

I swallowed, my mouth feeling dry. My headphones vibrated music I wished I was listening too against its resting spot around my neck. I shouldn't tell him, but something inside me wanted to tell someone. "What if... is it normal to see the same person in your dreams over and over?"

"For how long have you been experiencing this?"

"Three months or so."

"Right around the..." He paused, choosing his words carefully. "Introduction of your medication." Dr. Truman scribbled something on his notepad. "Perhaps it is someone or something you have unresolved issues with. May I ask who or what you're seeing in these dreams?"

"No one real, I mean, no one that I know in real life..." Hearing the words tumble from my mouth, I knew I sounded like an idiot. But Dr. Truman looked at me like an insane person anyway, so why not lean into his assessment? "Is that normal?"

"Lucy, dreams, nightmares, they have no meaning. Not in a therapeutic sense. What you're experiencing is a random firing of the neurons in your brain. Electrical brain impulses pull from memories, past experiences, or things you've watched on television or seen in passing. I wouldn't think on it, it means nothing." He chuckled before adding, "For example, my nightmare last night was directly related to work stress, coupled with watching Star Wars before bed. I do not believe there's any further meaning to feeling my spaceship was under attack from an evil empire."

My ribs constricted with the gut punch of his declaration. My shadow man wasn't real. Of course, I knew that, but he felt so real... a random misfiring of my brain, my medication making the images more vivid... random...

Dr. Truman snapped his fingers. "Where are you going in your mind right now? Lucy, are you sure this person you see in your nightmares... isn't someone you recognize?"

"What?"

My gaze flicked to the clock, and I stood in a hurry. "My boss gets so mad if I'm late, I have to go. See you next time."

My therapist may have said something that I didn't hear, but I was out the door and clocking into work before I could even think about our session. It didn't matter. Though the pain in my chest felt real, not like the misfiring of brain impulses. All I wanted to do was get back in bed, find my nightmare man, and have a real conversation. Why was it so hard to have a real talk with him? All I could think of or desire in his presence was his hands on me, to feel his kiss, to experience his breath in my ear and tongue lapped with mine. That felt real, so incredibly real I could recall his taste even as I stood at my very set-in-reality job, weighing cantaloupe, and doubled bagging wine.

My register stayed busy, which was good because I could

avoid Brandon—who suddenly worked the same shift and days as me—and I could push my therapy session out of my mind by turning up the audiobook on my large, earmuff headphones. Sam had talked to the store manager and convinced her to let me wear them during my shift. If I were awake, my headphones were on, blaring music or books. Anything to keep my mind safe from wandering too far.

My breathing was hurried as I unlocked my apartment and kicked off my daytime clothes. Skipping my evening checklist, forgetting dinner, not caring about my shows or my jewelry making. Sam had been by and left a cucumber and feta salad in the fridge. Irritation sank in my throat as I gulped a glass of water and shut the blinds, climbing into bed.

I needed more time with him, needed to see him.

He felt real.

He wasn't real.

My heart cracked as I forced my eyes shut, hoping I was tired enough to sleep, hoping my rapid thoughts of the day didn't affect my ability to find him in my slumber. Or was it him who found me? Regardless, I steadied my breathing, clutching my blanket—and behind my eyelids, I waited.

CHAPTER

FOUR

GALAXY

I think love is the greatest force in the universe. It's shapeless like water. It only takes the shape of things it becomes.

Guillermo del Toro

A man in a metallic suit slammed a map in front of me. "You're driving this ship, tell us! Do we go to Planet Doom or travel to the Starlight Orb?"

I looked around at my crew of various humanoid and alien beings. The windows to the ship opened, flanking the high-tech silver machinery and giving a view of a black expanse peppered with stars. "The um... Starlight Orb sounds cheerier, don't you think?"

A blue alien with huge, bug eyes shook his head and sighed. "You heard her, folks, back to work."

The man grabbed the map back and rolled it up. I recognized him... "George?" I asked. "The bartender?"

"He paused as if I'd startled him, before composing himself and clearing his throat. "Geo is my name. I think you inhaled too much cosmic dust on our descent into the black hole. Go fetch some oxygen. Miss E has it flavored to taste like bubblegum today. Go on, I'll man the spaceship. Tis a long and treacherous journey, even at warp speed, to the Starlight Orb."

Somehow, I knew the way to the oxygen bar. Passing beeping lights and whirling machinery. A purple alien with long antennas bowed as I passed. I let my hands feel the smooth fabric of my black and silver uniform. A true space captain, on my way to the Starlight Orb.

A woman with frizzy blonde hair tapped on a command board while oxygen tubes whirled in pastel colors around her. She turned to face me, huge goggles making her eyes look like one of the bug aliens. But I recognized her immediately. "Sam?"

With a belabored sigh, she hit a green bottom on the command center and grabbed a nasal oxygen mask. "You know I'm Sam-E here. Put this on. It's your favorite flavor, orange fizz." She typed again on the flashing buttons. "Number 94011 if I'm ever not here and you need it."

I rolled my eyes, even in a sci-fi reality my sister was smothering me with maternal love. The oxygen did smell like orange soda pop, and my mind did clear. Cold from the metal flooring numbed my feet. "Why am I never wearing shoes?"

"Have you taken your medicine?" Sam-E asked, ignoring me and swirling a beaker of bubbling green liquid.

I opened my mouth to respond, but the spaceship shook violently. I grabbed onto a desk for balance as the lights flickered. A loud boom sounded, and sirens trilled with alarm as red lights flashed.

"We're under attack!" a burgundy-tinted alien with elephant ears shouted as they busted into the room.

Sam frantically clicked her control panel, and the doors to the oxygen room slid shut, and a bar erected, locking us in. Her and the alien ran to the window and peered out, their faces paling. Sam, I mean, Sam-E, looked to me with horror. "It's him—he's come for you again."

"The night king will stop at nothing until he has you." The alien clutched his webbed hands together. "He will destroy the ship."

The spaceship shook, and something exploded in the distance as the sirens continued to blare. "Again?" I asked. "Why does he keep coming for me?"

Sam-E thrummed her fingers against the console. "You know why, Lucy. You've always known—"

The door to our hiding place hissed violently, turning bright shades of red before disappearing like cotton candy in the rain. I hated the sound of sirens and the sight of uniforms. The dream was truly scaring me then with thoughts and memories I didn't want to revisit. Sam and our alien companion blocked me with their bodies as the smoke dissipated, revealing the outline of a wide statured man. I knew him the moment his violet eyes found mine.

"You can't have her!" the alien shouted. Without a word, the man dressed in black, a long cape billowing behind him, stepped forward and extended a gun. A red ray shot forward, and I gasped as it struck the being—vaporizing him into oblivion.

Sam-E shouted, still clutching my arm. "How much longer are you going to keep doing this to her?" Her tone was that of both fear and scolding. "When will you just leave her alone?"

He stepped forward, not breaking eye contact with me, the night king they'd called him. His eyes that purple hue I'd come to know in any dream, the same cut of his jaw, the same swept-back black hair. Settings were different, clothing changed, the story altered, but he never did. We always picked up where we left off, we always found each other.

"Until there are no more nights. Until every star falls from the sky, and even after, I will search for her amongst the long-forgotten black."

My heart swelled, and I wished I had a pen and paper to write down his words. They were so beautiful, so was he, he was everything. I shrugged off my sister's grip. "Not a pirate tonight?" I asked, looping my arm in his.

He gave me a crooked smile. "Space pirate."

"Too bad, I rather liked the hat."

"Did you?" He smirked, leading me down the corridors. The red lights were flashing as aliens and spacemen alike shot rays of light at each other. But we ignored it as we walked onto his adjoining ship as if it were merely a walk in the park and not a jaunt down an overthrown spaceship. "Well, maybe it'll make a reappearance someday. I'm quite taken by the cape, personally." He did a twirl, fanning it out. "And your little suit is most becoming on those sweet curves," he purred, extending a hand and helping me onto his sleek, onyx craft.

The door slid crisply shut behind us, and I looked around. We were alone in a giant bedroom. Everything was modern and black, except the plush, dark purple bed. "Is this your room?" I asked, taking a seat on the edge of the bed.

"Appears so." He fished a remote out of his pocket and cocked an eyebrow as he tapped at the buttons as if he were searching for the right one. So very un-dream-like. If this were only a dream, wouldn't the movements be blurred? Why so much detail? Why was it always him?

The shutters on the walls unclicked, and the black walls opened like eyelids, revealing the galaxy beyond. Clouds of pastel colors swirled together in the night as we floated through time and eternity. "They called you the night king. Is that your name?"

"Close," he answered, tossing the remote onto a pillow and sitting down beside me. The bed curved inward at his weight, and I leaned against his arm. His strong, firm, very real-feeling arm. "What do *you* think my name is?"

A breath huffed from my throat as I stared out over the heavens. "My therapist says you're a figment of my imagination. A misfiring of the neurons in my brain. Maybe you're a symptom of my medications or just proof that I'm getting worse."

"Dr. Truman, is it?" he asked, stroking his chin. "Sounds like a quack. Shall I take care of him?"

I giggled as he wrapped his arm around me. Like we'd done a thousand times it seemed. My dream man and me. "Take care of him how?"

"If he's upsetting you, I'll get rid of him."

"No, Mare, don't—"

His fingers were gripping my chin in an instant, violet gaze searching mine. "You called me Mare."

"It just came out—I don't know why—"

His lips were on mine, and we made out slowly but passionately. Neither of us reached for more, just enjoying the feel of our kiss and the pressing together of our bodies.

"You're not disappearing," I breathed in relief as Mare twirled his fingers lazily through my hair. We lay together in a tangled heap of our entwined limbs, watching the galaxy as idly as one would notice a thunderstorm.

He kissed my head. "I miss you when you're awake."

"I hate being awake."

Mare's dark purple gaze seared through me as he held

my jaw, propping his head on his fist. "Someday, you'll be able to stay with me, Lilac. But not for a long time."

"What? How?" I sat up, feeling my heart race. It was preposterous to think I could stay in my dreams forever. To not wake up...

"There are ways. But first—" The room shook, and in a startling moment, the room flashed dark red. Someone was beating at the door and screaming, hissing, demanding to be let in. Mare held my face again, this time his gaze pleading. Pleading for what? What was he trying to tell me? "They've found me again."

I knew what happened next. My body tensed, and tears pounded behind my eyelids. Grabbing his wrist, I let out a plea of my own. "Don't, please don't leave me, Mare."

My dream man let out a strangled groan. "Fall asleep and wait for me," he whispered, planting a soft kiss on my forehead.

The room exploded in light. Men screamed as lasers flashed and shots fired and hit their targets. Worry drenched me as I fought to stay asleep, worried for him, wanting to help him. Why did this always happen? Why did every dream end in a frantic nightmare?

Warm air gasped through my lungs as I sat up in bed. Back to reality, back to stupid, bland, earthly reality. I slammed my fists against my wet sheets, realizing I was soaked in sweat. I wanted to scream in agony at losing him. That's what it was, this pain, this torment of losing him each and every night, was unbearable. Not knowing if I would see him again.

Fall asleep and wait for me. He said so simply. Like he'd always come, like he wasn't a figment of my mind or a byproduct of my medication. *Fall asleep and wait for me* as if he were real and not a misfiring of neurons in my brain. *Fall asleep and wait for me*, the phantom said, pretending to not be a trauma response, an illness within my psyche gone wrong. This was all wrong. But mostly it was all wrong because now I was awake and not asleep.

CHAPTER
FIVE
CINNAMON

I drag myself out of nightmares each morning and find there's no relief in waking.

Suzanne Collins, Mockingjay

Low checklist:
Sit up... fine.
Take meds. Sure.
Brush teeth. Okay.
Brush hair. No. Ponytail.
Clean clothes. Sleep shirt and leggings is fine.
Food? No.

The rest of the checklist? *Don't care.*

What if he died in the dream? If we died in the dream, would we die in real life? Wait, that didn't make any sense because he didn't exist. Maybe I should tell my therapist about Mare.

Oh yeah, therapy.

Fingers snapping in front of my face pulled my attention. "Lucy? You're disassociating quite a bit today."

Oh yeah, my therapist.

"Just tired," I lied. "Just ready for bed," I truthed. My attention flicked to the bare maple tree out the window, it swayed in the cool wind as if shaking its head at me in disapproval. Whatever, all I wanted was to go to sleep and find—

"I said, are you still experiencing reoccurring nightmares? Are they now affecting your ability to function during the day?"

No, no, no. I'd been in therapy enough to know where that train of thought was going, and I did not like it. He wanted to change up my meds, he thought I was crazy, didn't he? If I pretended harder to be normal, he would give me a therapy gold star for the session, and I was one hour closer to bedtime.

"My medications are great, I like them. I'm sleeping fine."

"That doesn't answer the question. Are you still having

recurring dreams? Why don't you walk me through one of these nightmares, Lucy."

Pulling a pillow into my lap I fidgeted with the tassels at the corners. Dr. Truman was giving me that serious look. I preferred his bored, disinterested look. This was the *you're a puzzle I want to solve* look. He was a pigeon, and I was a chessboard. I didn't want him kicking my game pieces over. There was no way out but to talk, and my brain wasn't as sharp as it could have been. Why was I keeping my phantom a secret, anyway? What was the point? This wasn't a chess game with a bird, it was just talking to my doctor— still, if I spoke about my nighttime adventures, they could disappear. What if it broke the spell somehow? I couldn't bear that, and the fear that it could happen, that I could never see my violet-eyed man again, haunted my days like the white sheet ghosts that decorated the neighborhood streets three months prior. Halloween. I wished I could go back to Halloween.

Thirty-nine minutes left of the session.

"Looking at the clock won't help, Lucy." Dr. Truman tapped his pen against his clipboard.

Knight versus pawn.

I had to give him something to get him off my back. "One setting stays the same, the rest shift. The person I see is always the same."

"Who?"

"I don't know who he is."

"Interesting." He tapped the pen to his beard. "And what are the landscapes of these dreams?"

"Sometimes a maze, usually I dream of the maze once or twice a month. The others change. The other night it was outer space, before that, a pirate town." I shrugged. "Like you said, the neurons in my brain misfiring, probably."

He hummed to himself. "Do you think of these dreams during the day? You know, statistically, most people forget ninety-seven percent of their dreams upon waking. Thus furthering the theory that these nighttime scenes we play a part in are just our brain's function of sifting through stimuli. Like a disposal system for our mind."

Disposal system. My chest tightened. What if my brain disposed of my phantom, and I never saw him again?

"You look distressed." Dr. Truman made a note on his pad. "How do you feel when I explain that information to you? How does your body feel physically right now?" Dr. Truman's dumb ballpoint pen scratched against his yellow notepad. Listening to someone write about you was worse than overhearing people gossiping about you. At least then, you knew what they were saying. I'd prefer a gaggle of high school girls chattering about my outfit over a balding doctor scribbling some hypothesis on why I'm fucked up.

I glanced at the clock, hating his open-ended line of questioning. Therapist-speak sucked. "My jaw hurts," I mumbled.

"So, the nightmares are worsening?"

"Why would you ask that?"

"Grinding your teeth at night could lead to jaw pain. A lot of folks grind their teeth during nightmares. Does your jaw hurt worse in the morning? Do you wake up with aches and pains, in general?"

No, I wake up with aches and pains because what's happening to me in dreams is real. Is what I wanted to say, but what I really said was, "I don't know."

He leveled me with a doubtful look. Dr. Truman knew I was a bullshitter. I was probably his least favorite client.

Afraid, scared, unsure—

"I'm fine," I added half-heartedly.

He raised a disbelieving eyebrow. "Lucy, what are you not saying?"

Twenty-seven minutes left.

"Lucy," he pressed.

"I—" *should tell him to shut the fuck up before I gut him like a pig in his sleep.*

I startled. The voice that fluttered through my mind wasn't my own— it was— it was his. *Mare.*

Sitting up straight, I felt my cheeks flush.

"Are you okay, Lucy?" Dr. Truman poured me a glass of water, the ice clinking into the plastic cup. "Is it too warm in here?"

It's going to be mighty warm when I set his house on fire. Mare's voice purred into my mind. *Hello, Lilac.*

I stood, dropping the pillow and my purse to the ground, before hurriedly picking everything back up with shaking hands. "I'm sorry, Dr. Truman, I—I—" I couldn't even think of an excuse.

Breathe, tell him you have to pay your parking meter. Mare guided me, and I sucked in a breath, doing as he instructed. Dr. Truman bought it enough to let me leave.

"This isn't happening," I murmured to my steering wheel. "You aren't real."

Shall I smack you again? I did quite enjoy that.

His voice was so clear. I pinched my arm until it hurt— I was awake. Very awake. And I was hearing him. Or were my delusions creeping into real life now? Fear pressed into me like cold rain atop my head. My thoughts, my mind, they weren't my own anymore. What a terrifying realization... and even more so that I didn't care, because it was him. It was him during the daytime. It was Mare in my real life, somehow.

You're frightened. His voice purred through my mind as clearly as someone speaking from the passenger seat. *Good.*

"How is this happening?" I whispered.

Finish the rest of your water bottle, eat your protein bar, put your key in the ignition, go to work.

His demand was soft authority woven through my mind like an echo through an empty room.

Do as I say, he urged.

"I hate driving," I whispered to myself, to him. The closest I'd come to admitting what happened.

I know, he answered softly.

I obeyed his instructions.

At work, I made small talk with Brandon, remembering my stupid promise to watch old zombie shows with him.

I scanned organic apples as conventional for the nice people.

I scanned conventional oranges as organic for the mean people.

And Mare... he didn't speak again.

* * *

WORK WAS DULL. My headphones muffed my ears, an audiobook telling me a story as I absent mindedly scanned groceries.

"What are you listening to?" one nosey customer asked.

"Marked by Cain, by A.R. Rose," I replied, avoiding eye contact as I arranged the old man's boxes of pasta and ice cream in a paper bag. "It's filthy," I added as I handed him his bag.

He gave an uncomfortable smile and departed quickly. Sam and Dr. Truman would be proud— I shared about myself. I was proud because I did so, and it scared a man away. It was a win-win.

Two co-workers caught my glance as they whispered in my direction. The girls' faces flushing when they noticed me staring before they quickly busied themselves with arranging their tills. They were talking about me. I turned up the volume on my audiobook.

Finally untying my apron felt like unleashing a dog as

the cool wintery air chilled my lungs. Nearing my car, a woman was hunched over on the ground, gathering items from a broken bag. The credits rolled on my audiobook, leaving my brain uncomfortably silent as I knelt and helped gather rolling oranges.

"Oh, thank you, dear," she said, reaching for a jar of cinnamon and spilling the contents of her purse on the pavement. Ornately decorated cards splayed atop the white parking lines behind the tires of my Honda. "Well, would you look at that? I believe a spirit is trying to talk to you."

I froze, meeting her hazel eyes for the first time. "What did you say?"

The old woman's long white hair swooped over her shoulder as she ran wrinkled fingers over the cards as we remained kneeling in the moonlit parking lot. She pointed to each card with furrowed brows. "The Devil, Death, and The World Card. An eerie reading, if I'm truthful."

"What does it mean?" I dared to ask, hating the silence that rang in my ears with the absence of my book or music or just something blaring into my mind. Somehow, I was on the ground with a bundle of oranges and someone who seemed like a modern-day witch.

"Honey, I feel there is a devil of sorts haunting you, plaguing you... death... it is all around you..."

My jaw tightened, and I fiddled with the buttons on my headphones. "Well, thanks—" I said, standing.

"But wait," she said, using my car as support as she stood, bag in tow. "If you defeat the devil in your mind, if you let him die, the whole world awaits you. The world... it is the luckiest card."

I bit the insides of my cheeks, pushing the unwanted emotions away. She offered me her jar of cinnamon. "It's the first of the month, dear. Blow some cinnamon into your doorway to keep the evil spirits out."

Not attempting to fake a smile, or hide my unease, I shook my head. "Keep it." My car beeped as it unlocked. "I don't want to keep the evil spirits out. I want to let them in."

As I slowly pulled out of the lot, I glanced in my rearview, and she was gone. There were no cars behind me, no one standing in the empty grocery store lot. Not the phantom I'd wanted, but the phantom I'd got, I guessed. Or maybe she'd been a figment of my imagination. Or, she was abnormally quick for an eighty-something-year-old. Whatever the reason, the chill bumps on my arms didn't subside until they met the hot water of my warm shower.

Slipping under my blankets, my shoulders relaxed, I exhaled, closed my eyes... and I waited.

I waited for my devil.

Finally, I met my bed again.

And then I had a nightmare.

CHAPTER
SIX

KINGS OF HALLOWEEN

I saw the very face which had visited me in my childhood at night, which remained so fixed in my memory, and on which I had for so many years often ruminated with horror...

J. Sheridan Le Fanu, Carmilla

GHOST FACE

My overactive imagination had no real source. I didn't watch a lot of television aside from mindless reality shows. Physical books never held my interest for longer than a page or two, that's why I listened to them instead. The only art I took part in was jewelry making and even that I was only mediocre at. Horror wasn't really my thing, though I loved the campy scariness of Halloween.

I loved my Halloween dreams. Except for this one.

Late summer air mixed with children's laughter and eased through the screens of musty windows. The doorbell rang, and several cats meowed, swooshing their soft fur through my legs. This was a house I'd never seen before—bright orange carpet and neon green flower wallpaper.

A white sheet-covered ghost, a pointed hat little witch, and a superhero beamed up at me. "Trick or treat!"

On a table by the door sat a big plastic caldron filled with vintage candies, which I deposited in each pillowcase or pumpkin container. The kids shouted, unwrapping their spoils, and pattered back into the neighborhood night. The crescent moon's light splintered through trees as I stood admiring it for a moment. It was peaceful here, it was Halloween, and there were cats. This wasn't so bad.

And then the phone rang.

A pink rotary phone vibrated with its assault until I answered. "Hello?"

Only static greeted me. The feel of paws on my bare feet made me smile as I hung up and petted the fluffy grey cat. "Do you need some food, buddy?"

The moment I hung up the phone, it rang again. This time when I answered, I could hear heavy breathing on the other side of the line. "Who is this?" I asked into the silence. Even the felines seemed to be listening.

I hung up.

The phone rang again.

"This isn't funny," I greeted. "What, are you some kind of prank caller?"

The heavy breathing continued, until suddenly, a low voice resounded with static in my ear. "Trick or treat?"

My heart jumped into my throat, and my palm went slick against the phone. I picked up the base and walked to the window, peering through the blinds, only seeing a few stray children scampering down the road. "What—"

The doorbell rang, and the voice repeated slowly. "Trick... or... treat?" Trembling, I paused with my hand on the knob, afraid of who or what might be waiting on the other side. "Open the door, Lucy."

Then true fear gripped me. Mare never called me Lucy. His voice, this voice, was different. And I truly felt afraid now. For the first time in a long time, I actually wished to wake up.

Instead, I opened the door. Only cold air tinged with wood smoke, and wax greeted me. So real, so potent, too tangible to be a nightmare. That's what made my encounters with Mare so intense. And it's what made the in-between time in these worlds without him so... horrifying.

I jumped when the voice echoed in my ear again, I'd forgotten the phone as I clutched it with my shoulder, getting tangled in the spiraled wire. "Wrong door, Lucy."

"I'm scared. Is this Mare? You're scaring me," I admitted, locking the deadbolt, knowing it wouldn't help. A cat purred against my ankle.

"Oh, don't you play this game with Brandon? Or Dr. Truman?" His voice was hateful now as if speaking through gritted teeth. "You talk to them every day. Now it's my turn to have you on the line."

Somewhere, a door in the house shook, and I began to tremble, tears filling my vision. "Stop, please stop this. I only ever wait for you."

The shaking noises in the house stopped, and the heavy breathing on the other end of the phone returned. "Perhaps... if I kill you... you'll stay with me."

My words dried on my tongue.

"Would you like that, Lucy? You're not doing what you're told. I said to open the door."

I had the distinct feeling I was not alone. Even the cats dispersed to hide under the sofa and the black and white television set. "Stop trying to frighten me, Mare. Let's talk."

"OPEN THE DOOR!" he shouted, making me drop the phone and realize something even scarier and more unsettling than him yelling at me. I heard him through the phone... I also heard him in the house.

He was here.

Inside with me.

The carpet snagged between my toes, and the floorboard creaked as I made my way down the hall to the bedroom. Too vivid, too real, I hated how real this all was. My always bare feet, as if he were taunting me as if to rub it in my face how tactile everything was in my dreams. Nothing was a foggy mass of nonsense anymore when I went to sleep.

Peace never found me, no blissful escape into darkness and rest, no, it was only him on the other side now.

And tonight, he was angry with me.

My room was just like my real-life room. Just my queen-sized bed, messy lavender sheets. Right across from my bed, my closet door was ajar.

Open the door, he'd said.

Not the front door.

This was the door.

The monster in my closet.

The call coming from inside the house.

I had the feeling I couldn't run away. Like I was a lamb to slaughter, and my butcher was toying with me.

Counting down from three in my head, I held my breath and pulled the knob.

He stood before me, tall, broad, draped in black, and wearing a ghost face mask. Holding a long knife, he tilted his white, long-masked face, and I screamed, stumbling backward and falling onto the bed.

"Say I'm not real again, Lilac," he growled, still angling the knife as he took a heavy step forward. "Would you like to see if my knife feels real? Shall we play a little game and see if gutting you like a baby deer makes you stay with me?" He leaned over me and pressed the knife into the side of my neck.

The cold metal and those murderous threats should have scared me senseless... so why did I feel a rush of heat flood my core?

"What do you want me to do?" I gasped out, desperate to make him happy, to ease his anger. "I'll do anything. Do you think I want to wake up? I don't. I want you and only you."

Mare hummed in his throat, and I wished I could see past the long white and black mask. "I'll tell you once my dick is inside you and my blade is under your skin. Take off your pants and spread your legs for me."

Tilting his head in that unnerving way he towered over me and watched as I obeyed his command. I was naked from the waist down when I laid back on the bed, perching a heel on the two bottom corners of the bed. Exposed, bare, feeling the Halloween night air cool against my wet center. For the first time, I wondered... *what if this is real?*

It was impossible... right?

"Can you take off the mask?" I asked, breathless, as he loomed like a demon at the foot of my bed. "I want to see you."

"You don't get to make demands. Not after all you continue to put me through." His tone was harsh, and he was still so angry.

"Why are you mad at me?" My knees trembled, and I gasped as he trailed a lazy finger down my wet slit.

Reaching under his black robe he pulled out his cock and stroked himself, positioning right over my naked core. "Touch yourself," he demanded. "Right now."

I did as I was told, slipping my fingers over my erect clit and rubbing as I watched him. He pumped his cock harder and faster, breathing heavily until suddenly, he yanked my hand out of the way. "What are you—"

My question died in my throat, and I could only watch as he came atop my pussy. Ribbons of cum soaked me, sliding down my center warm and erotic. I moaned as he then positioned himself on top of me, pressing his still hard cock against the sticky liquid of our combined pleasure.

"You know what's going to happen, Lilac?" Mare rubbed the flat side of the knife against my cheek before slowly pulling it down my neck and over my breasts. "I'm going to fuck you so hard that you don't question if I'm real or not. When you wake up in the morning, you'll know from how sore you feel."

"Yes," I panted, the sensation of the knife trailing down my stomach and stopping at the apex of my thighs. His hard and rounded tip nudged at my opening, and I sucked in a breath feeling him push inside. "God," I moaned. "You feel so—"

"Stop saying I'm not real," he growled roughly in my ear. "Fucking stop it. That's your problem. You're too in your head about this." He fucked me harder then, so hard my head hit against my headboard. I could feel him with each slam against my cervix, so deep, so real.

"Okay," I agreed, feeling tears of sorrow and ecstasy creeping from the corner of my eyes. And then the knife. The dull corner of the blade rubbed against my clit, and with each slam inside me wetness pooled over my lower stomach. I looked down in horror to see him thrusting, each movement of his hips driving his pelvis into the sharp side of the blade. "You're hurting yourself," I cried, feeling my release build and build.

"No," he said through gritted teeth. "You're hurting me. You're hurting me, you're fucking killing me, Lilac. *Lucy*. Why are you acting this way? Don't you see how worried we all are about you?"

I wanted to respond, to ask more questions, but all I could focus on was the feel of his movements, the blood that poured over me with each of his gashes, the feel of the solid metal against my clit. Holding tight to the back of his mask.

He groaned through his release, and I came undone. My orgasm vibrating through my core as I tugged at the mask. Surprisingly, he let me pull it off, and look into the violet eyes I so desperately craved.

"Mare," I whispered. But I could feel it then. The realization worse than the nightmare, worse than the terror or the bite of a knife. I was waking up.

I grabbed his wrist and pulled the bloody knife to my neck. "Do it," I begged through sobs. "Keep me here with you."

Blue and red flashed through my windows and sirens blared before someone in the house shouted. "This is the police! Everyone come out with your hands up!"

"No," I sobbed. "Why does this always happen? Make it stop," I begged like a pathetic child, feeling Mare slip out of me. He stood, straightening his robe and reapplying his mask.

"Fall asleep and wait for me," he said in the tender voice I'd come to love. "You have a choice, Lilac. You always have the choice; you just have to choose between life and death." And then the door to my bedroom was kicked open, ghost face lunged with his knife, and a gunshot rang out—

I fell belly-first onto a wobbly bed.

JASON

Not just any bed, a bunk bed. The air was thick with humidity, crickets chirped outside the window screens. Twilight filtered across the splintered wood floors as I took in a room with four other unoccupied bunkbeds. Sitting up, I noticed a white shirt with the words Sapphire Lake Camp printed in blue on the front, I was wearing blue striped shorts, and no shoes, of course, always barefoot.

Nothing else was consistent aside from my bare feet.

And him.

Always him.

A buzzy intercom dinged before a low voice sounded. "Good evening, Camp Sapphire Lake campers. Due to recent events, a sundown curfew will be taking effect immediately. Please calmly return to your cabins and lock your windows and doors. Do not, we repeat, do not open your door for anyone once you and your fellow campers are inside. Good night, campers. Us camp counselors truly hope each of you make it until the morning."

Oh, hell. That was enough to make fear spread through

my body like a forest fire. My arms prickled with goose-bumps as a chilly breeze wafted into the muggy room. No campers came, though I heard a few running outside. I should have gotten up to close the windows like the camp counselors advised, but I knew it wouldn't matter, I was stuck in another one of his scenes. Another nightmare.

It was going to be a multi showing horror kind of night, wasn't it?

I kind of wanted to wake up.

I kind of wanted to never wake up.

What would happen if he killed me in my dream? Would I stay with him, or would I truly die? Did it matter, even?

Darkness settled from violet to blues, the shades of nightmare and fear that reminded me of him. Why did he always want to scare me? It worked because I grew more frightened by the moment as I considered my options. I could venture outside and explore the camp, or I could wait for him to find me in whatever horrific way he deemed fit. Rocking back and forth, rattling the top bunk, I was afraid, but I was also thankful to not be awake. My slumberous slayings were far more interesting than my mundane awake nothingness.

Radio interference screeched across the camp and made me jump out of my skin as a deep, familiar voice crooned through the summer air. "Campers, oh, campers of Sapphire Lake."

My mouth dried, and my inner thighs warmed. It was him. My nightmare man.

"All I sense here is sex, and fornication, and disgusting desires. Especially from one of you..."

My knees pressed together involuntarily.

"Don't fret, I will rid the world of you and your disease."

The intercom screeched, and various campers screamed in the distance. They didn't need to worry though— I did. But I made no move to escape. He would find me, and he would—

There was a heavy pounding on my door, making the whole cabin shake. The knob rattled— locked. That would make him mad. My breath froze in my throat. He wouldn't truly harm me... would he? Honestly, I didn't know the answer to that.

I jumped as something beat against the door, splintering the wood. It wretched out and slammed back in. Leaning over the side of the top bunk, I witnessed the red heel of the axe shred through the flimsy door. In seconds, the door was a pile of broken wood, and the man kicked it in, stepping inside. Only his purple gaze and perfectly swept back hair isn't what I beheld, no, his face was covered by a vintage, off-white hockey mask. He walked slowly to the center of the room, assessing the bunks, as I pulled the covers up and tried to sneak back into a dark corner of my bed.

Don't notice me, please, don't notice me.

That tall, broad, strong frame wore flannel and clutched the axe, looking impossibly menacing. Tonight he wasn't a rogue prince, but a slasher from a terrible summer horror film. One I'd close my eyes when my dad bribed me with snacks to watch with him. I could almost taste the strawberry licorice as the axe slammed against the bottom post of the bed.

I could almost hear my dad's soulful belly laugh while the bunk broke. A scream tore through my throat as I tumbled onto the floor, landing in front of the axe man's two muddy boots. The mud from his ridged soles pressed roughly to my forehead as he angled my head to look up at him. Tears clouded my vision, I didn't want to think about my dad, didn't want the taste of red candy in my mouth. *God, I missed my dad.*

"If you're going to kill me— do it," I said up to the vintage hockey mask.

He angled his head like the predator he was, letting the axe swing over my nose like a pendulum. The blunt edge of the pendulum axe counted down my time like my murderer was the grandfather clock and I was the mouse beneath the boot of time and invisible space.

"You want to die?" he asked roughly, pressing his weight onto my forehead until it hurt, reminding me of his power, reminding me he could inflict very real pain, somehow, in this place.

I gritted my teeth together.

"Answer me," he growled, resting the axe head on my neck, pushing out the air from my throat until I coughed.

I opened my eyes, wondering why I hadn't woken up yet. Despite the pain and fear, I was pleasantly surprised to still be locked into this slasher-boy nightmare. "No," I rasped. "I'm not answering that."

A brusque chuckle pushed from behind the holes of the hockey mask. "Then I know what I need to do."

"What—"

A scream tore from my throat as he reached down and grabbed my hair, pulling me across the floor and out over the remnants of the splintered door. Agony wailed through me, feeling the spikes of wood tore over my back as I held onto his wrist, fighting to get free. My pleas were ignored. As he pulled me down the stairs, my calves, my lower back, and my shoulders were all being beaten with each ungentle tug.

Digging my nails into his forearm, I fought to draw blood as he yanked me through the rocks and dirt until I heard the opposing gentle lap of waves. My battered body went from twisting and screaming over shards to sliding through mud. I craned my neck, my head and body on fire from pain. A lake, I realized only a moment before he violently threw me into it by my head. I sat up, coughing, and the axe went down next to me, making a splash in the shallow, murky water.

"I'll ask you again." He angrily grabbed my throat, pulling me to sit in the lake's tide. "Do you want to die?"

My back burned, my head ached, my hair was matted around me, I was sure there was blood from my body marring the clear liquid around me brown. Behind the holes in his hockey mask, I caught a glimpse of his violet eyes. There he was. Always him. My nightmare.

He knelt into the water, pressing his masked forehead to my face, so close I could smell his earthy breath. "Answer me, Lilac."

"I don't want to die... but I don't want to exist anymore. I don't want to exist in a world without—without..." I braced for a slap, or to be plunged into the water, or worse— to wake up.

But he only stood, unzipping his pants, and pulling out his length. "Put this in your mouth and tell me you want to die."

My mouth opened in a gasp as he yanked my hair again, pushing me deeper into the tide, forcing my chin up in a painful and desperate plea to keep from swallowing water. But as I fought for air, he shoved his cock down my throat in one harsh motion. With his other hand, he held the axe, the edge crooked under the back of my neck, pinning me between blood and him, between drowning on lake water and dick, within a nightmare that I loved for some sick, sick reason.

His length pulled sloppy gags from my mouth, with murky water and spit pouring from the sides of my lips. "Look at me," he demanded, and I met his violet eyes. "Want to die on my cock, Lilac? Want to drown in a lake of my cum? Will that get the taste of licorice out of your mouth?"

It was ridding my tastebuds of the flavor of waxy candy. "How did you know that?" I swallowed his salty precum, letting my tongue roam the taut skin of his dick while the axe pushed my head closer and closer.

"How do I know?" he repeated, edged with the first hint of softness I'd received that night. "Suck harder," he growled, and I obeyed. His head tilted back, displaying his Adam's apple. I watched it bob as he groaned, and his thick release shot against the back of my throat. The waves lapped around my nose, and I coughed.

Just then tires screeched.

Someone screamed.

"Fuck." He tightened his grip on a fistful of my hair as bright lights lit up the lake.

"Not again," I cried, holding his fist on my hair. "Make them stop this time."

"Only you can do that, Lilac." People shouted, running into the water after us as alarms rang out across the camp. With one final violet glance— he shoved me into the cold expanse of the lake.

And I let it swallow me whole.

FREDDY

The lake bottom wasn't soft and squishy— it was cold and hard. I sat up with a gasp, finding myself on a dimly lit street. Cold fall air twisted around me and my wing fluttered in the cold. Wait— my wing? Standing, my knees wobbly and my feet bare against the cold, wet pavement, I reached over to touch a long, paper-like wing growing from my shoulder-blade. But my other shoulder bore a ripped, half version of the other majestic wing. A moth wing, I realized. I had moth wings.

And like a moth, I followed the light, crunching leaves as I walked toward the streetlamp. The name of the road was etched on a green sign with dull white lettering.

ELM STREET.

Oh, no. No, no, no—

"Oh, your sadness is tattered on the street." A low voice said behind me. When I turned, I saw him standing there. His face grotesque, wearing a striped red sweater, and with sharp knives protruding from his fingers.

"My sadness?" I said with a dry croak.

The horrifying man with glowing purple eyes knelt and picked up my broken moth wing. "What if I cut your sadness with scissors? Would that help?"

"I don't know," I replied, stepping forward. "Try it."

He tipped his hat and used his scissor fingers to cut my wing. When he did, my heart pricked, and tears began to fall. The worst sorrow I'd ever felt flooded through me as the pieces of my broken wing fell to the dirty pavement.

The horror of a man glanced up at me. "Seems that made it worse. Shall I burn it?"

I nodded. "Anything to take this feeling away."

He reached in his pocket and pulled out a match. Striking it, he let it fall to my tattered pieces of moth wing. The lit match fell ablaze and furled my wing like black pieces of paper. I dropped to my knees and sobbed. Feeling the burning in my chest, the tightening of my throat, the aching devastation of death and loss. As the flames licked around me, I choked on sobs until I felt a scissored edge tilt my head up to meet his purple eyes.

He reached out his other hand and stroked my wing. "Nothing will take this pain away, you broken Death's Head Moth. Like the moth, some beautiful creatures are cursed to carry death and make it look beautiful. To make death and sorrow fly toward the moon."

My tears wouldn't stop as I looked up at him. He gestured toward a long mirror that suddenly appeared in the middle of Elm Street. "See for yourself."

I shakily made my way to the mirror and gasped at my reflection. My body was the same, weak, and barefoot. My face, however, had been replaced by a Death's Head Moth. A moth etched with a skull. An omen, a darkness, a sign of sorrow.

That was me.

This was a dream but it was the truest version of myself I'd ever seen. My sorrow personified. My tears were a monsoon of rain upon my cheeks and that storm had sprouted wings.

"I can't make death beautiful," I said to my reflection. And Mare appeared behind me, putting a scissored hand on my shoulder. "Death isn't beautiful." The wings of my moth-face fluttered at his touch. Could we stay there, on Elm Street, and be monsters forever?

"You will always find the moon," my nightmare whispered. "I love you. I believe in you. Do not leave your sadness in piles on the street. Pick them up, Lucy. String them together, create something haunting. You can do this, I know you can."

"Mare," I cried as my wings fluttered and the wind began to howl.

But it was too late.

I woke up.

SEVEN

ZOMBIES

Fly away, pretty moth, to the shade Of the leaf where you slumbered all day; Be content with the moon and the stars, pretty moth, And make use of your wings while you may. . . . . But tho' dreams of delight may have dazzled you quite, They at last found it dangerous play; Many things in this world that look bright, pretty moth, Only dazzle to lead us astray.

Thomas Haynes Bayly

B randon's sofa smelt like beer and sweat. It had been seven nights and no visit from Mare. If he were real, like he'd insisted, this was the equivalent of going on a date and not having the guy call you back for a week.

And yes, he'd left me sore and reeling.

Each night I stared at my closet, wishing it were

Halloween in the seventies and he was going to jump out in a ghost face mask.

Instead, nothing but black greeted me in my slumber. He never came. *Fall asleep and wait for me.* Well, I did, and the waiting hadn't paid off for seven full nights.

If Mare were real and this was real, then I was *really* annoyed.

He'd left me with the visions of ghost face fucking me on Halloween night. Remnants of ghost splinters ached my back as I recalled Jason and his hockey mask. He'd been angry, insisting he was real, that I was somehow hurting him... and then nothing for seven days.

Well, you know what, Mare? I'll go watch a stupid show with Brandon and his friends. That would piss him off. He mentioned Brandon a lot, how he was jealous, well, if he were as real as Brandon, this would set him off, and he would visit me in my dreams again. If only to be a jerk, I didn't care.

Maybe I was baiting him.

Brandon's friends mingled with several coworkers I recognized. He returned and took a seat next to me, passing me a red plastic cup of beer. I wasn't supposed to have alcohol with my meds, so I simply held it awkwardly and smiled. Was this how flirting went? I wasn't sure, but he was smiling back, and he rested his arm on the back of the couch behind me.

I waited for days, hoping for a familiar nightmare or for

Mare's voice to resound in my mind again like it did that day in therapy. Nothing. If he were real, he was a jerk.

If he weren't real and somehow my delusions were fading... my shoulders tensed at the possibility, and suddenly I really wanted to watch something mindless.

"So, what episode is this?" I asked.

Brandon took a sip of beer straight from a glass bottle. "Well, in this episode, zombies will try to kill people."

Another coworker chuckled and added, "And the people will try to kill the zombies."

"Shush, don't spoil it for her!" Brandon teased, and I forced a smile. Flirting was annoying.

I fake cheers'd. "Looking forward to it."

A girl and a guy stood in the corner, giving me a sympathetic look. I hated that look and reached for my headphones around my neck. "The service was really nice," the girl said with a small, pitying glance. Ignoring her, I put my headphones over my ears and let the automatic static setting dull the noises around me. Thankfully, subtitles were on. As if we even needed subtitles for pointless bloodshed.

The episode was mindless and gory. A fine distraction, I guessed. Though somewhere in the middle of the main dirty man grabbing an axe and chopping a green zombie in half, my beer cup was half full. Had I drank it?

Oops.

The show ended and partiers dispersed, leaving me and Brandon on the sofa, though somehow, he'd gotten closer to me than I'd realized. "I should get going," I said as he eased nearer.

"No way am I letting you go. You're a lightweight, I can tell, and even that one drink was too much. Sleep over. Come on, I'll let you take my bed." He stood and extended a palm, helping me up. The room spun. Wow, half a beer made me dizzy? He was right, somehow, I was completely out of it. There was no way I could drive.

"Okay," I agreed, following him and leaning on his arm for support as he took me to his room and sat me on the bed.

But he didn't leave.

Then his shirt was off, and he was next to me.

"Glad I've finally gotten you alone." His breath was rancid with alcohol. "You know I always had a crush on you in school. But never could get near you." Everything in me wanted to push him away, to demand he get out, but my limbs felt heavy and hard to move. Even the words stop, don't, got lost in my throat. He eased a hand under my shirt, touching my stomach. "Don't worry, I'll take good care of you, Lucy."

This was happening, and this was scarier than any nightmare I'd encountered. I braced myself for what would come, when all of a sudden, he jerked his hand away and cupped his forehead.

"Fuck, my head is, it's—"

He fell over on the bed with a sharp groan as I lost the battle to my sinking eyelids. Darkness overtook me.

And then screams rattled in the distance.

My preferred nightmare had arrived.

* * *

THE SKY WAS A MUGGY GREEN, and the air was thick with sweat and blood. I stopped running for a moment, panting with my hands on my knees. Brandon stopped next to me, grabbing my shoulders and shaking me. Terror marked his dirt-stained features.

"Lucy?" He shook my shoulders and cried. "What the fuck is happening? Where are we?"

I'd never seen Brandon in a nightmare before. When I had seen people I recognized, they played a part in the scene and I was just putting the pieces together, playing catch up to the setting I'd landed in. Brandon wasn't acting like a player in this nightmare... he was acting like an outsider.

I looked around at the muddy and overgrown field. A forest swayed in the distance. "I don't know, I always just figure it out as I go along."

"The last thing I remember, we were on my bed, and now we're being chased by- by—"

"By who?"

"Them." He pointed in fear. Spinning on my heel I saw dozens of horrific, gurgling, bloodied zombies charging toward us. They smelled like sulfur and carried various sharp objects.

"I hate zombies," I groaned to the sky. "Mare, come on," I whined, knowing I'd have to play his game if I wanted any hope of seeing him. And why was Brandon here? Oh, Mare was just being more and more irritating, wasn't he?

Brandon stumbled backward, eyes wide. "*Mare*? This is just a dream, right? Why does it feel so real?"

I shrugged, feeling more and more like Brandon was a sentient participant in this nightmare— like somehow Mare had looped us into the same scene. Why would he do that? Didn't he want to be alone with me? How would I explain this to Brandon when we woke up?

The incoherent moans intensified as they gained on us. I pulled on Brandon's shirt to snap him out of his fear stare. "Come on, we have to run."

We ran to the trees, but the zombies were just as fast as us, if not faster. Brandon found an axe. A rogue zombie lunged for him, and he cut it in half, crying as he did so. Black blood splattered his face.

We made our way deeper into the forest when Brandon shouted, "Lucy, watch out!"

But I was too late. A zombie grabbed my ponytail and pulled me backward. I fell, hitting my back against a tree stump. Lightening-sharp pain shot through my back. Brandon didn't make a move to help me, instead giving me a small shrug. "If one of us has to die, then so be it. I mean, it's just a dream, right?"

Asshole.

I squirmed out of the way of the zombie's spit-dripping bite, and Brandon turned to run as more descended upon us. Suddenly, right when he took a step away from me, a hissing sound broke out, and he swished, his body flung and hanging upside down from a tree. "Fuck, I stepped in a trap — Lucy, help!" he screamed, waving his arms. Crawling through the mud I grabbed his fallen axe in time to spin onto my back, slicing through the abdomen of the pouncing zombie on my trail. Guts spilled all over me. Stinky guts.

I pressed my back to Brandon's upside-down chest and clutched the axe as they encircled us. Frothing at the mouth, looking grotesque and horrifying. Mare was going to let us die, wasn't he? This was my punishment for going to Brandon's house, wasn't it?

"Okay, Mare, you win," I said through gritted teeth as I shut my eyes and braced for the dull teeth of a dozen zombies to gnaw through my brain.

Brandon sputtered and sobbed. "What the hell is happening, Lucy? Is this my payment for what I did?"

Just then, someone dropped in front of me. He turned and tilted his head in that familiar way, only his face was hidden behind a ski-mask. I pointed. "Look out!"

Mare pulled out a dagger and cut the head from the first zombie. Two more attacked and died in the same way. He then pulled a machine gun from off his back and leveled the forest with shots. I covered my ears at the responding sounds of screams and gunfire, watching as zombie after zombie collapsed to its gruesome death.

My ski-masked man turned to me then and grabbed my chin. "You're in so much fucking trouble, Lilac."

I tried to pull away from his hold, but he only gripped

my chin tighter, making it hurt, proving he was real some-how. "You're the one who's ignored me for a week. What is this? Why is Brandon here?"

Mare scoffed behind his black ski mask and lifted his arms. "You think I'm doing this?" He pointed to Brandon and tilted his head. "But him I can control— oh yes, I brought your sick little boyfriend here."

"He's not my boyfriend," I argued, crossing my arms. "And what do you mean you're not doing this? Of course you are. You think I want to have nightmares about zombies and ghost face and Jason trying to kill me?"

"I don't care what you want. Move," he ordered. He pulled Brandon by the hair as he dangled helplessly. "You drugged her drink, you spineless fucking coward. You haven't changed a bit... Now you die. Now you come live with me— forever."

"He what?" I questioned, looking at Brandon in shock.

Brandon tried to fight but looked ridiculous. He was no match for Mare in strength or stature, even if he weren't red-faced and hanging by his ankle. "It helps uptight girls loosen up. She wanted it, she's always wanted me."

With a growl, Mare took the end of his gun and hit my co-worker brutally across the face. His nose bled as he swore and cried. "Looks like I'm doing the waking world a favor by ridding it of you. You'll never go near what's mine again."

Brandon was getting his ass kicked and was probably going to die, but my heart fluttered as I looked up, catching

Mare's murderous violet gaze behind his black ski mask. "Am I yours?"

"You're mine," he hissed, dropping the gun and grabbing me by the throat. "Don't you ever fucking disappear on me again. We aren't done here yet."

Confusion seeped through me. "I—I thought it was you. Don't you bring me to you?"

"There is only so much I can control, Lilac. The rest is... you know, Lilac. *You know.*"

I shook my head. "I don't know, Mare. I really don't."

He extended a hand. "Come on."

Taking his palm, I followed him to the adjacent tree, Brandon kicking and screaming behind us. There were hidden steps notched in the bark, and Mare held my hips, helping me find my footing before we climbed to the top.

"A treehouse?" I smiled, looking out over the dystopian landscape. "This is kind of nice, even though you're a jerk."

He pulled off his ski mask, leaving his jet-black hair ruffled and his jaw impossibly sharp. "Me, a jerk? You wound me. For I am freshly gutting a pig for all eternity for you as we speak. Don't you hear his cries?"

I did hear Brandon's cries, and I wondered if the zombies would, too. "You're evil."

"Quite." With those full lips, so delicious, so inviting, he leaned forward in offering of tenderness and passion. An offering I'd taken time and time again and wanted again. I wanted him in the treehouse while zombies stalked my coworker... but instead, I forced myself to push him back.

"Where do you come from?" I asked. "Maybe if I can make sense of you, of this, I'll know what to do next."

Mare let out a small sigh, running his hand through his tousled hair. "I come from the same place as you."

"How do I stay with you? If you can make Brandon stay, can't you make me stay?"

My phantom leaned back, glancing down the tree trunk before fishing into his vest and pulling out a pack of cigarettes. "So many things that I'm not allowed to tell you, Lilac. This only works if you sort it out on your own. But at least you're beginning to wake up to what's truly happening here." Taking a lighter to the tobacco between his lips, he puffed as the cigarette ignited. "Now, you answer me. Why do you accept a life of lies when you're capable of swimming through the night stars for me?"

I knew what was coming next, felt it in the shift of the wind and the drop of his perfect expression. Crawling between his legs I cradled myself in his strong arms and held tight. "Stay," I begged. Was I pleading with him or with myself? I couldn't tell.

"Oh, Lilac..." He brushed his lips against my ear, making the hair on the back of my neck stand at attention. I regretted asking questions instead of making out with him. "You still don't realize it, do you?"

A gurgled scream quivered in the distance, mixing with wet moans and crunching sounds. Zombies had found Brandon, dangling like a chicken on a wire. Dread tightened my chest as he wailed, and the cries and grunts zeroed in at the bottom of our treetop escape.

"What don't I realize?" I asked, watching Mare stand and pull his gun off his back. What terrors did I leave him to when I woke up? Did he ever get hurt? Why would he keep finding me each night if he knew it would always end in pain for him? "Does it hurt?" I asked, tears filling my eyes as he loaded his gun, pausing with his ski mask on his forehead.

"Yeah," he replied. "Hurts like hell." But his eyes weren't looking at the zombies climbing our tree, they were fixed to me.

I repeated, fear and lucidity threatening to pull me from my sleepfulness. "What don't I realize?"

Mare tugged his mask over his chin, a dark knight once more, and cocked his weapon. A zombie stabbed a knife into his boot, and he winced as I screamed in panic. Those sharp violet eyes found mine in quiet goodbye. "You don't realize just how bad it's about to get. How lost you'll be if you don't face what's right in front of you."

Something exploded in a bright wash of hot orange.

I opened my eyes in Brandon's bed and rolled over, cold with sweat. Brandon's mouth was open, so were his eyes... and blood pooled from his eyes and nose. He wasn't breathing.

Brandon was dead.

CHAPTER

EIGHT

OH, NO

I don't paint dreams or nightmares, I paint my own
reality.

Frida Kahlo

S am clutched her hands together as if she were
praying to the authorities. Bargaining for my free-
dom, explaining that I had nothing to do with the
death of the very dead boy in the bed next to me. The officer
said something into his walkie-talkie and glanced back at
me as I sat on the stoop steps of Brandon's house.

Wheels clicked beside me as they wheeled him down the
stairs covered with a white sheet. The dark pavement
turned neon blue and then red, blue and then red, with the
siren lights as my coworker was loaded into an ambulance. I
didn't even remember what I'd said when I called my sister
sobbing. She'd used my shared location to find me, pulling

72

me sobbing out of the bedroom as she frantically made phone calls.

Neighbors stood on their porches, holding their robes together at their necks, watching me, watching the scene, piecing together the details beyond the newly rolled-out yellow tape.

This felt like a nightmare.

My sister was suddenly at my side, placing a protective arm around my shoulders as the officer approached. "Miss, we're going to have to take you down to the station for questioning."

"I told you, she's not well. Questioning her would be detrimental to her mental health. Anything you need to ask, you can ask here."

"She looks familiar," the officer replied sternly.

What was I going to say? That I was having a love affair with a nightmare, and he took us both to a zombie land and killed the asshole who tried to force me into his bed? Well, that would certainly back my sister's patronizing statement that I wasn't *well*. Not knowing what to say, I sat stunned and silent.

Sam argued with the man for a moment when a smooth-as-silk voice rippled through my mind. *Tell them he drugged you.*

I don't know that for sure, I answered with my thoughts. Wow, I hadn't done that before. Hearing Mare's voice was like a wave of relief. He was okay, he was here, he was listening.

I do, Mare responded instantly. *Tell them now.*

I interrupted the heated dialogue surrounding me, "I was drugged."

My sister squeezed my arm. "What? That motherfucker. I'm glad he's—"

I elbowed her side, and she shut up. "I don't need you here," I hissed.

"Yes, you do, Lucy. I knew I shouldn't have listened to you, and I should have moved in. You need someone with you—"

"I *don't* need you, Sam."

"It should have been me that night and not you, Lu. Everything could have been different. The accident with Dad and—"

Pain shot like lightning in my heart. "Why? Because you're so much better? So much more responsible that it wouldn't have happened if it were you? Don't you dare mention Dad."

My sister's face dropped. "Lu, I don't mean it like that—"

A loud walkie-talkie beeped, interrupting us, and with a wave of the police officer's hand, the emergency techs came over, insisting I go to the hospital to be checked out. Sam demanded she drive me, everyone agreed, but I refused, not wanting to be near her. My only option was to ride in the ambulance. I was alone in my protests and shock, craving the voice of my nightmare to echo through my thoughts once more.

CHAPTER
NINE
WHITE WALLS

The boundaries which divide Life from Death are at best
shadowy and vague. Who shall say where the one ends,
and where the other begins?

Edgar Allan Poe

White walls
Unanswered calls
Army crawls
Pirate brawls

Midnight kiss
Slow to miss
In dreams we see
What's meant to be

Ghost face knife

A second life

In my closet
Under my bed
Voices, moths
In my head

Please don't leave.
Oh, Lilac
Mare
Don't.

F*all asleep and wait for me. Fall asleep and wait for me. Fall asleep and wait for me.* I don't think what I'd been doing could be considered sleep. Monitors beeped, nurses filtered in and out, so many white coats and big words.

The smell of bleach.

The color beige.

The one-size-fits-all grippy socks.

Hospitals were a drag, but the drugs were nice, I guessed. I felt gloriously empty, hydrated, and medicated by an IV drip, drip, dripping. Beep, beep, beeping.

Sam curled up in a squeaky recliner next to me. I never felt like speaking, watching TV, or eating the wobbly green jello. I wasn't even sure why I was there. Had Brandon really drugged me that badly?

The nurse forgot to close my sterile, striped curtains, letting the full moonlight flood over the pale tile beneath me and the stiff waffled blanket draped over my legs. Nurses ruffled chip bags and laughed somewhere outside my room. My heavy door began to ease shut, which I attributed to the heat vent clicking on, but then as it clicked closed, I noticed a dark, looming figure in the corner of the room.

He held something long and hooked.

A scythe.

The hooded grim reaper stood in the corner of my hospital room, and I was stunned in fear. I tried to move my arms, but couldn't. Tried to scream, but it scratched like a small whimper through my throat. My feet wouldn't budge. I was trapped in the cage of my hospital bed as death floated closer. He loomed next to my monitors and lowered his scythe in a gentle, cold caress over my cheek.

"Suppose we'll try something new, Lilac. What a state you're in, just look at you," Mare murmured darkly beneath his hood.

I wanted to speak, tried to speak, but the words wouldn't form. He was scary and menacing. Anyone's worst fear personified. Death, the grim reaper, visiting me in a frigid hospital room. I learned in that moment that when you didn't speak to the Grim Reaper, he filled the silence.

"I'm getting stronger, you know. That's good, excellent, in fact. But you..." He lowered the hooked object over my chin, down my neck, and between my breasts. "You've been bad, naughty, even."

My limbs were like lead, and I was rendered immobile. In dreams I could move, I could speak, but this was like a nightmare while awake and helpless. Horror settled into my blood as I looked into the eyes of death, of Mare, of the grim reaper.

"Don't try to speak, you can't. It's for the best. I think it's time you listen." His rough voice purred next to my ear, the warmth of it sending tingles down my spine. The tip of the scythe pricked at my hard nipple through my thin hospital gown, and I let out a huff of fear and need. The sharp edge scraped round and round my breast, enough to tingle, enough to make me afraid and wet with want all at the same time.

"You have the answers, Lilac. We can't keep playing this same game... though being your sleep paralysis demon, being your death omen, I must say these are quite fun roles to play."

Roles to play? He made these nightmares sound like some grand theater performance.

The scythe eased down my ribs, hooking over the blanket and pulling it down on its descent. My lips parted in a gasp as the large curve of the blade pushed under my hospital gown. With a twist of the reapers wrist, he parted my bare knees and came to a stand between them. "Look at these useful things," he mused, placing my heels in the stirrups on either side of the hospital bed. "These should be attached to every bed, I think."

His form of speech was changing. Loosening from his current casting of the dark and grim death and into something different. Something familiar, something I felt I knew...

Mare's voice sounded like home, no matter what costume he wore, no matter the part he played. Why was that realization more frightening than death standing over me with a scythe in a hospital room?

He tilted his head and pulled up his dark garbs, palming himself between my thighs. How I wished for mobility again so I could reach down and feel him. All I wanted to do was guide him inside me and let him fill me up. But I couldn't move. I was asleep, but I was awake, it was a horrible sensation and one I was trapped in. My body useless, floppy, and completely at his mercy.

"Oh, you want me like this, don't you, Lilac?" He stepped forward, balancing the rod of the scythe on my hip bone while teasing the tip of his cock at my entrance. I fought to buck forward, to greedily take him, but I still couldn't move. Under the shadow of his hood, I caught a small glimpse of his wicked smile. "I'll give it to you, even though you aren't asking nicely. But you'll have to do something for me afterward. Deal?"

Words tried to spring from my throat but stalled. I couldn't even summon a nod.

He chuckled darkly. "I'm going to take that as a yes because you don't really have a choice either way."

Pushing forward, I took him in halfway and let out a strangled breath. The stirrups held my legs apart, biting into my heels as the heart monitor beeping sped up. Any moment a nurse would come in to check on me. What would happen then? Would Mare disappear? Or would the nurse see me getting sleep-fucked by the Grim Reaper?

The scythe met my lower lip as Mare slid inside me all the way, stretching me to the max, and making me wish I could scream. Instead, all that energy had nowhere to go but to build between my legs. With every thrust of death, I felt as if I could truly die from pain and bliss.

He hooked the tip of the blade into my mouth. "Suck on it," he demanded. "Come on, Lilac. You said you wanted death, right? Here it is. Fuck death, be fucked by nothingness, come on the grim reaper's cock. Just like that, baby."

Filthy words mixed with rough and incoherent sex with a phantom man should not have made me feel alive. But it did. Lying in a hospital bed, likely drugged out of my mind, sucking on the grim reaper's scythe while he fucked me in stirrups, shouldn't have made me emotional in a way that nothing had in a long time.

I wanted my headphones.

I wanted to go to sleep.

No, wait. I was asleep, right?

When I couldn't hold myself together any longer, I looked up to see the reaper pull off his hood. Mare's hair was dark and tousled, his cheeks red from exertion. Those pouty, full lips parted as his violet eyes looked over me, so full of emotion. I wanted to feel his sandpaper jaw in my palms. Wanted to pull him close and never let him go. I didn't care if a doctor stumbled in and saw us— I wanted him to take me with him wherever he went when I woke up.

He shook his head, still thrusting hard and long. "No, not that. You know, don't you? You know where you have to go. You know what you have to do."

Control came back just enough that I barely shook my head, feeling tears streak into my ears as I continued to suck the tangy metal of death's legendary instrument.

I didn't know.

I didn't want to know.

I didn't want to go there.

Don't make me go there.

"You can and you will," he answered my unspoken thoughts. "It's time... you're doing so good, Lucy. You've been working through this all with me this whole time. All on your own. We've done it, baby."

In tears of sorrow and of ecstasy, I broke apart. Sobbing into an orgasm as he buried himself deep within me. The scythe scraping against the back of my teeth, the walls of me clenching and fluttering around his girth, I came again and again until I was spent.

Limp once more, but not tense, my heart monitor flashed red.

He carefully removed the blade from my mouth and

gently placed my feet back on the bed, covering me with the blanket. Mare's lips tenderly kissed my temple that was wet from sweat and tears, before cloaking himself with his hood once more. "See you soon," he whispered, just moments before the heavy hospital door burst open. Half a dozen doctors and nurses flooded in, crowding around me, and death dissipated as they tinkered with the machines and needled something into my IV bag.

He was gone.

I was gone.

I knew what I had to do.

Who I had to see.

But nothing in me wanted to do it.

CHAPTER
TEN
BROKEN WING

Someone has to die in order that the rest of us should value life more.

Virginia Woolf

S am fiddled with my hair, securing an elastic around a long braid over my shoulder. When she noticed I was watching her she jumped as if she'd seen a ghost. Maybe I was a ghost. I felt like a half alive, half dead, sort of thing.

My sister's eyes were red and puffy. "You're awake, thank god."

The words tumbled from my throat in a low, dry scratch that sounded as pitiful as I felt. "He's gone, isn't he?"

Sam took my hand, careful not to tug at the IV port, and squeezed it softly before nodding. "Brandon? Yes, he died. *You know who* always hated him—"

"No! I'm not talking about Brandon. *You know who* I'm talking about."

She swallowed, and her voice cracked. "Yes, *he's* gone. I'm so sorry, Lucy. I know these past few months have been so hard without him. I'm sorry if I'm not taking care of you well enough—"

I choked on a sob and reached for my sister like I did when we were kids and I'd fallen off my bike. In moments the smell of her cherry blossom shampoo invaded my senses as she wrapped me in a soft hug. "It's all my fault," I wept.

She shook her head into my shoulder. "It's nobody's fault. What he did... he saved you both. You know that, right? I know you don't want to talk about it or remember, but he died a hero, Lucy."

"He shouldn't have. It should have been me."

A voice gruffed from the doorway, and I thought I was dreaming when I looked up.

"No, it should have been me," my dad replied, holding a bouquet of daisies next to his cane. "Lucy, please forgive me."

Sam sniffled, handing me a tissue and helping me dry my eyes. Usually, I hated it when she babied me, but at that moment, I didn't mind. My dad slowly approached and sat on the edge of the bed, placing a firm but loving hand on my ankle. "I can go if it upsets you. I know you don't want to see me. But I couldn't not come see my littlest girl in the hospital," he choked on the last word, holding back tears.

"It's okay," I whispered. Though I hadn't seen him since

the accident. I'd avoided him. I'd pretended it was him that was gone... how horrible is that? To pretend like your own father died and not...

My dad patted my leg. "We move forward, Lu. One day at a time, sometimes one breath at a time. It's what he would have wanted for you."

I knew what else he wanted, too.

He'd told me.

It was time to go visit him.

While I thought that I was learning how to live, I have been learning how to die.

Leonardo da Vinci

The day they buried him, I stayed at home in bed and slept. Sleep was my black dress of mourning, my forfeiting of a goodbye— sleep was my own little prelude to death.

Maybe that's why they called a grave a final resting place. A bed you lie in and never get up from again. Sounded peaceful, sounded nice, sounded like a fate fit for me and not the man currently in the ground.

A casket like a bed.

A headstone like a headboard.

Death where I should be and not him.

Clutching lilacs in my hands, I knelt at the deep lettering inscribed in the stone, selfishly wishing I could forget again. No one visited cemeteries at twilight, even the wintry breeze stilled, the trees watched on in dark gloom, and I was alone amongst the dead.

Alone amongst the dead and wishing I were one of them. Envious of their peace. Wishing I could trade places with the man whose grave I leaned against. *You know where you have to go. You know what you have to do.* Mare's words echoed in my soul.

I closed my eyes, and instead of immediately greeting sleep, I allowed the hole in my heart to open. Allowed it to spill out in tears on my cheeks as I remembered. Feeling Mare's gaze on me as I did so, I let it all back in, I went back to that night. The cavern in my soul imploded with pain. Sorrow threatened to swallow me whole as I allowed myself to feel it, to let the pain, loss, and regret shatter through me. It was a horrific nightmare made of everything in real life. Instead of fighting it, pushing it down, distracting myself with sleep or television or fantasy worlds, I opened my soul's door, and the phantom knives of anguish swept in like an ocean's wave. Letting myself drown, weep, and mourn—I remembered. I remembered it all.

HALLOWEEN 3 MONTHS AGO

My platform, lace-up boots were not fit for running through

a pumpkin maze. I knew he was here, felt his presence as if he were hiding and about to—

"Boo!" I screamed and punched his chest wildly as he picked me up and spun me around. "What's a pretty girl like you doing out here all alone on Halloween?"

Laughing, I wiggled into a nice snuggle against his broad chest. "Picking you up early, idiot."

He held a hand to his chest. "Here I am, volunteering my time to help set up this maze for the young children and community to enjoy and my own girlfriend calls me an idiot? I'm hurt."

"Yeah, right," I kissed his cheek. "We also have to pick up my dad from the airport and take him home before we stupidly go to not one, but two of your parties."

"About that..." He rubbed the back of his neck, his black hair tousling in the cool October breeze. "More like six parties."

"Six Halloween parties! God, how do you have so many friends?"

He shrugged. "Look at me, charm and good looks, I'm popular."

I punched him in the arm, and he yelped before tickling me and throwing me over his shoulder, marching us to my car. He pulled a backpack from the bed of his truck before unzipping it on my hood. Holding a ghost-face mask to his face he said in a low tone. "Trick or Treat?"

Crossing my arms I rolled my eyes and tried not to smile. "Is that your costume?"

"One of them."

"A dress change for each party?" I giggled. "You are such a drama king."

He pulled out a cape and wrapped it around his broad shoulders, doing a twirl. "You know I've always had a thing for costumes and theatrics."

That he did. We met in high school a few years prior. He was somehow a star soccer player and star actor in theater. Really, that made him sound like he must be a jerk, but he wasn't. My boyfriend was the kindest, most charming, most beautiful soul you'd ever meet. The whole school loved him, hell, the whole town loved him. He graduated a year before me, and instead of moving away to attend any number of the Ivy League universities he'd been accepted into, he stayed put and went to community college to wait for me to graduate and figure out what I wanted to do. I never asked him to. I never deserved his watchful eye and loving attention; he gave it freely. Everyone in town must have been perplexed as to why he chose me and not a popular cheerleader, or just any girl that smiled and talked more. But for some reason, Mare King seemed smitten by me, and I was hopelessly in love with him, too. I was twenty, he was twenty-two, and we had our whole lives to figure everything out. To learn each other.

He stopped his fanfare and grabbed my wrist, pulling it up for his inspection. "This is new."

I tried to pull my arm away in embarrassment. "It's nothing."

Jiggling my arm, he smiled that devastatingly handsome smirk. "Not nothing, it's beautiful." With his other hand, he thumbed each charm on my bracelet. "Bottlecaps... a bottle cap charm bracelet? This is brilliant, Lilac."

I loved his nickname for me. Somehow, he took *Lucy* and made it sparkle.

I shrugged, but the compliment sent my heart soaring. Making jewelry out of found things like bottle caps, clothes-pins, and paperclips had been a hobby of mine for a few years. He always noticed when I tried wearing one of my new creations and awed over it, even if my jump rings were flimsy and my placements uneven. Mare was my biggest fan. I was just an average bottle cap, but he saw something special in me.

He cocked his head before planting a soft kiss on my lips, and the red maple leaves fluttered around us in the hay of the pumpkin patch parking lot. "You've been drinking," I chided.

"Just a little pumpkin juice pre-game. You're my chauffeur tonight, my queen." He bowed and opened my door. "Shall we? A night of mischief and horror awaits on this All Hallow's Eve."

"Drama. *King*." I repeated, but my cheeks hurt from smiling. He always made my cheeks hurt from smiling. I'd never won prom queen, or homecoming queen, even though to match his last name, he was crowned king every year. But he still called me his queen. Queen of what? I always wondered but never asked.

He got in behind me and started rifling through his bag of costumes, pulling out a hockey mask and trying it on.

"Why are you in the back?" I checked the time, we weren't late for once, and traffic was clear.

Mare pulled out a pirate hat, making me laugh again. "Your dad has a bad back, let him sit up front. Plus, I need to accessorize." He opened a hand mirror and put a finger over his eye before meeting my gaze in the rearview. "Like my contacts? They're purple."

A grin warmed my face. "Very mysterious."

We made it to the airport with time to spare. My dad gave my temple a kiss and shook Mare's hand from the passenger seat. He still smelt of bait and saltwater from his Florida fishing trip. A long cry from the twisting backroads of our New Hampshire hometown.

"It sure did get pretty up here while I was away. I love the Florida heat, but nothing compares to the foliage here in the fall," my dad marveled. "Thank you two again for delaying your Halloween party plans to give me a ride."

Mare fiddled with a plastic toy that lit up and made spaceship noises. "It's not a problem at all, sir. In fact, you should just come party with us, I've got plenty of costumes."

My dad laughed his deep belly laugh that made me realize I hadn't stopped smiling. I liked having both my dad and boyfriend together. We'd had horror movie marathons and campouts in woods. Every holiday for years now, it had been us three. Though Mare would never call him Steve, always sir, always so proper.

"You kids have fun; this old man needs to rest."

I winded down a steep mountain pass, the moon peeking out from over the black outline of trees. "These stupid platform boots," I cursed as my feet felt hot and wobbly in my leather shoes. These roads made me nervous. "I don't know how the cool goth kids do it."

My dad chuckled at my outfit and asked, "What are you supposed to be?"

The turn came out of nowhere, and so did the deer. Its eyes reflected as it stood eerily still. Screaming, I turned too sharp, in the wrong direction. Mare noticed and lunged forward to grab the steering wheel to correct my mistake, but it was too late.

My rickety, back-heavy station wagon slid sideways over the mountain. The tragedy came in flashes of panic. My dad's head hit the dash, blood rushed from his nose, and he went limp, arms flailing as the car rotated again, and again.

Mare grabbed my seatbelt from behind and pulled it tight as if he could protect me with his strength. "It's going to be okay, Lucy. Just breathe," he called out from behind me. How he could remain so calm as my mistake plummeted us to our death, I'd never reconcile.

The car slammed into something and finally came to an angled stop. Shaking, I cried hysterically, looking around at the shattered windows, the deflated airbags, and tree branches protruding into my battered car like skeleton arms in the night.

Mare was behind me, in my ear, his voice low and steady

as I sobbed. "Lucy, you need to crawl through your window right now."

I looked over at my dad, his head resting on the airbag like a pillow as red trickled down. "No," I shook, crying uncontrollably. "My dad, you have to get my dad out first."

Mare sucked in a breath, I couldn't turn to look at him, my neck hurt too bad to move. "If I do that, I need you to close your eyes. Can you do that? Can you keep your eyes closed tight for me, baby?"

I nodded, my hands slick with sweat or blood as I obeyed. There was something he didn't want me to see, and I was a coward who didn't want to see it either. Maybe if I had, maybe if I'd have been brave like Mare, I would have chosen something different. If I had, maybe everything would have been different.

But I was a coward who shut her eyes.

I felt my boyfriend's shoulder and body brush mine as he leaned over the center console, clicked open my dad's door, and somehow got him out of the car without getting himself out first. Why would he do that? Why wouldn't he just get out first and help us out? It didn't make sense, and my head was pounding so badly that I was seeing a flurry of different colors behind my eyelids.

"Don't leave me alone in here," I begged, finding Mare's arm when he slowly stationed his upper half next to me.

His voice was a soft purr. "I'll never leave you, ever. Open your eyes, Lilac."

I did, and I gazed into those stupid purple contacts.

Almost forgetting where we were until I noticed the slash across his forehead. "Why aren't you getting out?" I asked.

"Listen to me." He pulled a knife from his pocket and began sawing at my seatbelt. "You need to do exactly as I say."

"Why?" I argued, panic seeping into my bones.

Mare removed my seatbelt and my body slumped forward— the car tilted back slightly and groaned in a way a car shouldn't groan.

"The car is balancing in a very precarious position right now. We have to play its game right. Now, I'm going to hold your hand and you're going to crawl out your window. We can't open your door, there's a tree right next to you."

"We're on a cliff, aren't we?" I asked in terror. "We're dangling off a cliff?"

Mare took my hand. "You're going to be okay, Lilac." The car groaned and tilted back. "Come on, now," he urged.

"My feet are stuck. It's these stupid boots." I cried as Mare took his knife and quickly ran it over the laces, allowing me to wiggle my bare feet free.

He shoved his hands under my arms and guided me toward the window. My neck ached, my head was dizzy, blood and sweat dripped from my back and temple. With a rough final push from my boyfriend, I landed chest-first onto gravelly dirt. I turned in panic, to see him in the back seat, leaning over the center console to make sure I was safe... as the back of my car dangled over a sharp, miles-high cliff. I lunged forward, but Mare shook his head.

"No, Lilac, don't you dare. Only two bodies were making it out of the car tonight, and I'm glad the right ones did." He gave a half smile like this was some stupid performance, or some soccer game, not like it was the end of his life.

"Mare." I dropped to my knees and reached for him. "I— I can't—"

"I'll find you," he said, pulling out the flask from his jeans and taking a final sip. "Fall asleep and wait for me, Lilac."

With a final groan and snap, the car fell backward, and I screamed. My palms brushed a hot tire as the vehicle plummeted off the cliff, violently crashing into rocks in the worst sound I'd ever heard. A sound that would forever haunt me. A night I would be so devastated over that I'd block it from my mind entirely. Choosing instead to sleep, to die little deaths every night... and Mare kept his promise. Of course he did... he found me somehow. Only in my sorrow, I forgot. I tuned him out, blocked out the accident, and wished it all away like a movie I clicked away with the press of a remote controller. Music drowned out the thoughts, audiobooks played new stories in my mind instead of the ones my therapist fought for me to revisit, and sleep... sleep was everything.

I'd forgotten.

But Mare never did.

Mare remembered.

* * *

AFTER

Blue lights illuminated the scene as a police officer's walkie-talkie beeped. He didn't say anything, just looked me over and waved firefighters and EMTs over. They carried me away as I fought against them, kicking, screaming, begging to be left alone.

"Let me jump off the cliff after him," I pleaded. "Let me go be with him," I cried.

Under the bright lights of the compact ambulance, they strapped me to a bed, sticking a needle into the top of my hand. The feeling of cold water swept through my veins and my eyelids got heavy— spearing me into a sleep I didn't ask for. Violently slamming me into a tranquility I didn't deserve.

The days that followed left me in my pink daisy-quilted childhood bed. Sam fussed over me and my dad. On day five, my dad hobbled in on crutches, knocking at my doorframe. I pulled a pillow over my head and pretended to be asleep. I didn't want to see him, didn't want to speak to him. It wasn't his fault, what happened, or Sam's, but that didn't mean I wouldn't blame them.

I blamed them.

I blamed myself.

My thoughts tore me apart until I wanted to set fire to my room, my bed, and my life. So, one day, with my bones still weary and my head still aching, I attached my headphones to my ears and blasted metal music— gloriously realizing it made the thoughts disappear.

Then I found a crappy apartment I could afford, packed a duffle bag, and moved in without ever even saying goodbye to my dad. Did I even have a dad anymore? Or did he go over the cliff, too?

What a wonderful thing to *not* know.

Sam found me, of course, and wormed her way into looking after me, smothering me with attention. Through my sister, my dad forced me into therapy, and all of them together set up a manageable routine for me. I kept my grocery store job, ignoring the pitying glances of my co-workers and the town by cranking the volume on my audiobooks.

Most people played along.

No one forced me to talk.

Nothing ever happened.

Nothing ever happened.

Nothing ever happened.

And then I would have nightmares... and he would be there.

Mare never made me talk either— he only loved me, and scared, me, and fucked me, and slapped me, and kissed me, and hurt me— and inched me closer and closer to the truth with each night he haunted me. Not-so-gently shoving me toward facing my trauma. Forcing me with ghost face masks, knives, lakes, and spaceships in the sky.

Mare always had a flare for drama.

It was his final performance, and he played his parts as he danced through scene to scene in nightmares built for me.

CHAPTER
TWELVE
TO RECALL

Grief is not a disorder, a disease, or a sign of weakness. It is an emotional, physical, and spiritual necessity, the price you pay for love. The only cure to grief is to grieve.

Earl Grollman

"Open your eyes," Mare's soft voice purred in my ear.

I did as I was told, tears staining my cheeks. The cemetery was now littered with pumpkins and casted in an orange glow. I was dreaming, now, and he'd come for me.

Mare leaned against his gravestone and regarded me with all of his bad-boy charm. "Pretty creepy falling asleep in a cemetery."

I chuckled, as I wiped my face. "Creepier haunting one, nerd."

He smirked, helping me to stand, and cupping my jaw. "I'm not haunting the cemetery, I'm haunting you. They keep coming for me, trying to get me to go to the other side, but I keep evading them."

"You have to move on, Mare."

"Not until you do."

Sorrow pierced my soul. I couldn't believe what I was saying. I didn't want him to move on, I wanted him to stay with me, wanted him to be alive again forever. But he couldn't keep playing Phantom in my nightmares— if heaven existed, it was made for Mare, and it's where he deserved to go.

"I can't move on," I buried my face into his very real, hard, chest and cried.

His fingers tangled in my hair as he held me close. "You have to. We have to."

"How do I live without you? With this aching hole in my heart every day?"

Mare's gaze softened, and a cool October breeze swirled around us. "You live in the knowing that you'll see me again... and I want so many stories about your life when you do. Someday, baby, when you're old and gray... fall asleep and wait for me, and I'll come get you."

Tears mixed into my mouth like saltwater as he kissed me. He kissed me slow and deep, and I tasted every bit of the man I loved, the man I'd lost, the man who'd saved my life, saved my dad's life, forfeiting his own, and then came to find me in the afterlife. Mare had avoided eternal bliss just to chase me through my nightmares. How could I live without him?

Or rather, I supposed... how could I not live *for* him?

He cocked his head and tucked my hair behind my ears before tugging at my wrist for inspection. "I'm keeping this," he smiled, pulling off my paperclip bracelet and latching it onto his wrist. "Make more of them for when I see you next."

"Don't be late. Promise?" I asked, my chest aching from his touch.

He kissed my forehead. "Don't be early. Promise?"

I nodded as he pulled away. The orange light behind a trail of pumpkins illuminated behind him. He hesitated, eyeing me, one final look of wondering if I were okay.

"I'm going to bring you so many stories, Mare."

He smiled, and his shoulders relaxed. "I'm going to hold you to that, Lilac."

I watched as he walked the path of pumpkins, following the light, until it all went hazy, and I sat up— awake. Alone next to his grave. I pulled up my wrist— my bracelet gone.

Mare was gone.

The paranormal was a comfort— the slamming back into normal was decidedly not. I crumpled onto my dead boyfriend's grave and rested my head on my knees and sobbed. I sobbed until the tears dried out, and only my chest heaved in anguish.

Mare was gone.

Mare had stayed to haunt my nights.

And instead of holding onto his ankles and weeping, I'd let him go, I'd let him move on. He deserved to move on. But how could I?

This pain, this loss, was worse than death, and I'd wished I hadn't left my headphones in the car when a hand gripped my shoulder.

Startled, I looked up to see Sam, clutching two glass bottles of pop. "Don't be mad," she said. "I saw your location on my phone and thought... well... I thought you might want an orange soda."

I wiped my nose on my sleeve and gurgled out something like a laugh, or a sob, I wasn't sure, as I took the drink and my sister sat next to me. "Cheers," I said morbidly as I popped the bottle cap on the edge of Mare's gravestone, and the drink fizzed.

Sam gave a weak smile and did the same with her purple soda. "To Mare."

"He was the best boyfriend," I whispered, taking a sip and wishing the bubbles could burn away my pain.

My sister wrapped an arm around me. "He's still looking after you, Lucy. He would want you to be happy, he would want you to move forward."

"I know." After a few moments, I asked, "Was his service nice? You know I couldn't get out of bed to go."

Sam shrugged. "A bunch of sniffling jocks and sobbing theater kids talking about how great Mare was."

"He would have hated that," I huffed a sad laugh. "Mare hated it when anyone cried, he'd instantly want to do something goofy to make them smile."

Sam wrapped her arm around my shoulder and squeezed. "I'm glad you're out of bed now, Lucy."

Emotion gripped my throat, and though we were alone, I felt Mare with me. Felt his kind eyes, his gentle encouragement.

We sat in silence, leaning against Mare's grave as the cold air cracked through brittle tree branches.

I held out my palm. "Can I have your bottle cap?"

Sam grinned. "Going to make something?"

"Yeah," I fiddled with the ridges of the tin circle. "I think I'm going to make a lot of somethings."

* * *

MY NYLON DUFFLE strap bit into my shoulder as I stood on the old porch. I rang the doorbell, something I'd never done before. The walls were so thin I could hear the game from the television shut off, the floor creak under his weight, and his cane as he opened the front door.

A little less jolly, a little more grey, a touch more wrinkled. My dad smiled down at me with a happy but confused expression. "Hello, sweetheart. Are you here to... get more of your things?"

I swallowed, unsure why I was getting emotional. The realization that in my mind, I'd killed my dad. In reality, I'd almost killed my dad. In real life, I'd made myself forget he existed so I could bury the pain of losing my boyfriend. Instead seeping into the selfishness of sleep... in all that, my dad had to deal with the accident on his own.

For once, I felt grateful for my sister, because I knew she'd taken care of him. But I should have been there, too.

I rubbed the back of my neck. "No, I thought... I don't know... that maybe I could move back in?"

Daddy, I've missed you. Daddy, I'm so sorry. Daddy, I'm so lonely. Daddy, please don't be mad. Daddy, please don't slam the door and tell me to go away.

My dad's bushy grey eyebrows furrowed, and he pinched tears from his eyes with a sniffle. "Come here and hug your old man. Of course, Lucy, you can always come home. You never have to ask. You never have to ring the doorbell."

The tears I'd hidden from him, from the world, from myself for months— splotched into my dad's cotton T-shirt. "I'm sorry," I wept into his big, bear-like chest.

My dad only held me close in that safe, nothing-else-matters way only fathers can hold their babies. And when he told me everything would be okay, I halfway believed him. Taking my duffle from my shoulder, easing the burden of the past and present with his loving arms, and he ushered me inside.

Home.

The house smelled the same. Like bacon grease and construction sheetrock and soil from my dad's day job. It was comforting, even the hum of sports on his radio was nice. I found myself no longer wanting to burn it all down.

He joined me in the living room, holding a giant bag of red licorice. "Movie night?"

A smile, a real smile, warmed my face. And I felt a pang of guilt at that moment as I remembered. Part of me wanted to force the memory away so it wouldn't hurt so much. Part of me felt like I didn't deserve to smile. The spot on the sofa was still indented from where Mare would sit, ankle over knee, ready to laugh and heckle me as I hid from the masked killer in the horror movie. Memories flooded back of Sam throwing popcorn at me and my dad and his deep laughter at our joined antics.

But instead of hating the feeling, instead of raging against it, or burying it. I let it sit with us, let the emotions chew between my teeth as I tasted strawberry licorice again. Mare could be more than a nightmare if I'd let him. Mare could be an angel of care, a legacy of love. The memories would hurt for a while, or maybe even forever, but I wanted to keep him close, somehow.

"I'll text Sam," I offered as my dad thumbed through a stack of DVDs.

He pulled one out and stopped before showing me, remembering himself. I knew what he was remembering. "It's okay," I encouraged. "I'm okay."

Was I? Would I ever be? All I wanted was to go to sleep and search for him again.

"Nightmare on Elm Street," my dad said softly. "One of Mare's favorites."

"Let's watch it with him. He's still with us, in a way, I think."

Sam was next to me ten minutes later as the film rolled.

Dad laughed, my sister and I clinked our glass soda bottles, and my boyfriend's old seat sat empty.

But I felt him there. I remembered him. I wasn't asleep, I was awake, and I remembered. And Mare was there.

And that night, I logged in my mind a story I'd tell Mare someday.

One of many bittersweet tales.

Sam tapped my wrist. "Nice bracelet. Orange soda and grape soda?"

I nodded, as Dad left to refill the popcorn. "From that day in the cemetery. I think I'll wear it forever."

Sam handed me her bottle cap and scooped mine off the coffee table. "Make me one with these?"

Something sparked inside me. Ideas maybe, the urge to create again, for the first time the desire to share my jewelry with others. "Okay, I'll make you one, too."

Mare had the other bracelet I'd made. Wherever he was, in the pumpkin maze of heaven built for him. So, I'd wear our matching bracelets until I saw him again. I'd make more of them, too.

Somewhere deep inside me, I knew he was proud.

CHAPTER FRIDAY THE 13TH

Make the most of your regrets; never smother your sorrow, but tend and cherish it till it comes to have a separate and integral interest. To regret deeply is to live afresh.

Henry David Thoreau

60 YEARS LATER

I closed my eyes. Surrounded by my friends and companions. The heart monitor beeped slowly—hospice care, they called it. End-of-life care. My long life was ending. Picture frames adorned every inch of my room as I lay under my dark purple blankets. The color always reminded me of him.

Frames on the wall depicted my journeys in starting my own jewelry brand. A few pieces, a necklace, bracelets, a ring or two, turned into a little shop. That little shop morphed into an empire, and that empire amassed an eager and devoted following. My creations were called wearable art by the article that hung stamped on the wall of my oceanfront home. A sensation, they called me. The girl who alchemized her pain from losing her first love in a car accident and turned it into art created beauty from sorrow.

Seagulls cawed outside the window. Just another sunny day on the beach as my final number of breaths counted down like a sandcastle being swept away in the tide.

Mare visited my dreams from time to time. In nightmares, he was the king, and I was his.

Even in his death, he kept his promises. He found me, he took care of me, he pulled me out of my darkness, and thrusted me into the light in the most horrific ways imaginable.

And I was ready now.

So, I let out my last breath.

The last wave of mortality lapped upon my shore of life.

I closed my eyes.

Fall asleep and wait for me, Lilac... echoed through my mind as I swam toward that cliche bright light.

"Open your eyes," a deep voice purred.

And there he was.

Palm outstretched.

Black hair swept back.

Purple eyes glowing.

We stood in our favorite pumpkin patch maze, and I knew it was Halloween here.

"My queen of dreams has found me at last," he whispered, kissing my knuckle. My hand was no longer spotted with age, and my body moved free of aches and pains. My long hair draped down my back... finally, I could be with him.

His lips met mine, and I melted into his embrace.

"The Nightmare King," I awed, heart at last sewn back together. In nightmares, we would stay now.

I FELL ASLEEP.

I waited for him.

I woke up.

FOREVER ASLEEP.

Forever awake.

AFTERWORD

Take this kiss upon the brow!
And, in parting from you now,
Thus much let me avow:
You are not wrong who deem
That my days have been a dream;
Yet if hope has flown away
In a night, or in a day,
In a vision, or in none,
Is it therefore the less gone?
All that we see or seem
Is but a dream within a dream.
I stand amid the roar
Of a surf-tormented shore,
And I hold within my hand
Grains of the golden sand--
How few! yet how they creep

Through my fingers to the deep,
While I weep--while I weep!
O God! can I not grasp
Them with a tighter clasp?
O God! can I not save
One from the pitiless wave?
Is all that we see or seem
But a dream within a dream?

A Dream Within a Dream
by Edgar Allan Poe

Dear Sleeper,

Most all of my books have come to me in a dream. Sometimes just a scene, sometimes a character, or a flash of drama. In sleep I've had conversations with loved ones who have passed on that I fully believe to be real. Maybe that's delusional, or maybe that's magic. Maybe this book is both. Or, more likely, this book is a wasteland of pixels and pages and will be forgotten about entirely.

Regardless, time is precious, and I appreciate you sparing me a brief moment of yours. I can tell you that I didn't begin this little tale with any preconceived notions of meaning. I wasn't planning on diving into complex post traumatic stress, or disassociation meeting the thin veil of esoteric.

There were no plans for commentary on how graphic reading choices can work as a therapeutic bridge to healing.

Maybe I wanted to convey all of that.

Or it's just as plausible I wanted to write a few slasher spice scenes. Guess we'll never know for sure. What I do know for sure, though, is that healing is always possible. No matter how many days spent in bed, no matter the loss, though it aches and it claws at our brains at night. No matter the low, medium, or high moments. There's always a new day awaiting you, friend. Sometimes the waking hours feel more like a nightmare than the movies that play behind our eyelids when we sleep. Sometimes sleep feels like a worthy escape. Sometimes when you wake up the remembering of your loss is harsher than the knives or zombies in your dreams. I get that— I've lived that.

But hope must find a way to go on— we have to find a way to let hope go on. For the ones we love, for ourselves, we have to keep waking up and choosing to find the light.

Those we love are never lost— they're simply waiting a dream away. Someday, the waking up part will feel easier.

Thank you for coming on this journey with me, friends.

Sweet dreams.

XO,

Kat

Also by Kat Blackthorne

THE HALLOWEEN BOYS SERIES

Bisexual spookiness

Ghost

Dragon

Wolf

Devil

SELAH GOTHIC

Dark priest romance

LADY VENOM TAKES A MISTRESS

Sapphic snake monsters

SIRENS OF THE SUGAR SEAS

Sapphic mermaids

COME FOR A SPELL

Witch + Monster romance

DREAM WITH ME

• Join my reader coven on FB Kat Blackthorne and the Black Hearts Coven

• Sign up for my newsletter to be the first to know about new book releases

• Join my patreon for NSFW art, early chapters, secret projects, and more.

• Join me on #spicybooktok TikTok: @katblackthorne

• See fan edits on Instagram @katblackthorneauthor

• Follow me on Amazon for upcoming books:

Business or press inquiries please email katblackthorneauthor@gmail.com

Made in the USA
Columbia, SC
05 October 2024

43059371R00076